THE CHOICE

Kathryn Jacques

ISBN-13: 9798579242617
ISBN-10: 1477123456

Cover design by: Katie Rasinski
Library of Congress Control Number: 2018675309
Printed in the United States of America

For Mom, Dad, Neil, David, Lisa, Louis, Kelly, Genevieve and Emily.

CONTENTS

"The hardest thing in life to learn, is which bridge to cross and which to burn."

–DAVID RUSSELL

CHAPTER ONE

When I woke up the morning of April fifteenth, I was convinced my number would be called in the Gamble and less than twenty-four hours later I would be escorted to my death. It would be a sacrifice for the greater good, to ensure the continuation of ROC and the last 50,000 survivors of the human race.

But I wasn't selected, Rey was. Rey, the boy I'd grown up with, who had been my best friend since we were six and who asked me to marry him so I wouldn't be forced into an arranged marriage of my father's choosing. Rey, the boy I realized I loved.

Even love can't stop the Gamble and his death nearly destroyed me, leading me to the toxic surface of the Earth, which no one had walked on in nearly a century after the nuclear fallout of World War III. I was going to the surface to die so Rey and I could be together again in whatever world exists after we leave this one.

Or at least that's what I thought.

There was once a time I thought I knew so very many things. I accepted the truths of the world as they were told to me. I put faith and trust in the people around me. Why shouldn't I have? Why would the people I love lie?

But they did. So many lies I am still trying to sort through them and navigate how deep they run. Those lies, and the people who spoke them, have hurt me and crushed me and picked apart my insides like parasites. They haunt me every moment of every day as I wade through a vast swamp of truths versus betrayals.

Now I know the real truth. That the nuclear bombs were a lie, the radiation never existed, and the people leading ROC; my own father included; have crafted a web of lies to suppress and control their own citizens. I still don't know what their end game is, but I don't ever want to be a part of it again.

Now I know that people live on the surface, they always have, fighting their own wars against their own enemies and tyrants, like Sawyer and Elijah and the rest of the League; a radical group who have made it their newfound mission to destroy me simply because I'm from ROC. I'm a Sub, and so therefore they hate me.

But now I realize those truths weren't even the hardest to handle. In fact, at this moment I have forgotten everything else that has happened in my life, a brief reprieve from the astounding madness born from decades of deceit. It's as if someone has hit a pause button on my world. The breath freezes in my lungs and I am left motionless in the middle of the dark woods.

For what feels like an eternity, no one speaks or moves or does anything other than stare at each other in dazed wonderment. A breeze rustles the trees, crickets chirp in the grass, but the heavy disbelief surrounding the three of us drowns all the other sounds out, as if we have been sucked into a vacuum, a black hole into where my sanity has also disappeared because this? This is truly insane.

I must be dreaming, or hallucinating or maybe I am already dead and this tortuous vision is payback for all the lives I've inadvertently ruined and the people I have murdered. Or maybe he's a ghost or I've gone totally nuts, the events of the past few weeks putting so much strain on my mind it finally snapped like a slender twig bent in half.

But regardless of dream or hallucination or shear lunacy, I know this can't be real. I watched him go into that chamber and I know there's no way out. People don't live after they've been chosen by the Gamble. Ever.

As I continue to stare, immobile as if suspended between reality and a dream world, Rey moves forward, his pale hair glistening silver-white in the light of the moon. Even in the near dark, I can see the brilliant crystal blueness of his eyes as they sparkle, wide and confused, mirroring my own. My heart wrenches in two with a stabbing anguish because all I've wanted is to see him again, see those wonderful eyes and golden hair. Knowing this is an illusion is torture unlike any other I have experienced yet.

Then he speaks.

"Kelsey?" It's only one word, only my name, yet it floats and flutters in the air between us like one of the delicate, stunning butterflies I now look for whenever I am outside. Coming from Rey's lips, hearing his deep voice again, I never realized how beautiful my name could sound.

"Rey... how... what... I- I don't understand," I stammer, standing less than two feet from my best friend. My best friend who is supposed to be dead with his ashes sealed in a wooden box imprisoned two miles below the surface of the Earth. Now I am close enough to touch him, to hug him... to kiss him once more. My eyes dart over his thin body, across his sunburned face, the rest of the world tunneling away.

Shock radiates through me like bolts of electricity, causing me to tremble and shake and I take hold of a nearby tree to stop myself from falling. Tears sting my eyes, though whether from sadness or madness or confusion I have no idea. "You died..."

"Kelsey," he says again, "how did you get out? How are you here?"

"You died," I repeat softly, unable to find any other words, my fingers digging into the bark of the tree as though it is all that teethers me to the ground. It's the only thing that feels real anymore as it buries under my fingernails.

"What's happened to you? I didn't think I'd-"

"You died!" I scream, my shrill voice shattering the quiet surrounding us.

Eyes large and round with disbelief of his own, face colorless in the poor light, Rey steps forward and clasps my shoulders. His hands are solid and strong, erasing any thoughts that a ghost stood before me. He's real. He's Rey. And despite all odds, he's alive.

"I escaped."

I reach up and touch the backs of his hands as they rest on my shoulders. My fingertips run over his rough skin, calloused and scarred from his work in the air ducts, and I guess from whatever he's done to survive on the surface. I can't believe it. I can't believe he is here, that I am touching him again. My eyes meet his as I search for answers. "How?"

"We don't really have time for this," Jax says as he moves to my side, almost protectively. I'd forgotten he was even here, his voice jolting me back to reality while he gently pulls me toward him with his injured hand, half mangled from a fresh gunshot wound. His good hand rests on the weapon hanging at his side as he glares at Rey with wary distrust. "We need to get back to the new compound before more of the League find us."

With his bandaged hand, the first signs of blood seeping through the fabric, Jax tries to take my wrist and guide me away. I shake him off and scramble back, closer to my friend. "Rey is coming too."

With a tight jaw, Jax refuses to acknowledge Rey, eyes narrowing at me instead. "He's a Sub."

"Seriously?" I spit, hands balling into fists. "This crap again? I'm a Sub! You have a freaking barcode on your wrist now too so by everyone else's standards, you're practically a Sub. What does it even matter what he is other than my friend?"

Jax's eyes flash with menace while he looks Rey up and down as if assessing an opponent. I'm reminded of how Jax looked at me the first time we met, how he wanted to just shoot me because he realized I was a Sub too and he hated me for it without even knowing me at all. After all this time, so little has changed.

"That's different," he says. "You're different."

"No, I'm not, Jax. I'm not leaving him so he's either coming or I'm staying. Which is it?"

Calculating the two choices I have offered, Jax's lips tighten into a thin line. He then pulls a small handgun from the back of his jeans and holds it forward, grip first, offering it to Rey. "You know how to use one of these?"

"No, Jax he's never-" I begin, but am cut off.

"Yes," Rey says with confidence. Taking the weapon, he expertly checks the magazine to find six bullets left, slides the rack and flicks off the safety. And he does all of this with the expert precision of someone who has handled weapons for years, which is impossible because they are illegal inside ROC with the exception of the Gendarme.

For the second time in a matter of minutes, I'm left dumbstruck, mouth hanging open. "Where did you learn how to use a gun?"

Running his tongue over his chapped lips, Rey lifts his eyes until they catch mine again. They're the same clear blue flecked with bits of grey that I always remembered and thought I'd never see again. Yet now they seem different; alien; swirling with something I don't understand, a cool harshness so foreign to Rey. I falter backward slightly, fingers wrapping into my mother's heart-shaped necklace as if it's the last thing left that can offer any sort of comfort.

He grinds his teeth and tousles his dirty, tangled hair as if deciding what secrets to share. "Kels, there's a lot I'm going to have to explain and a lot we need to talk about, but your... uh... friend is right, we need to get out of these woods first. Given all the gunfire I heard, it's not safe here."

The snap of a branch causes us all to flip around. The shadows shift and change, the dark outline of a figure advancing toward us.

"Get down!" shouts Rey, yanking me sideways as he fires two rounds at the attacker, who quickly twists behind a tight cluster of thin birch trees. Jax fires too, the pop of bullets echoing in the night.

A muffled grunt and a dull thud come from the underbrush.

"Is he...?" I ask, not really wanting an answer either way.

"No idea, but let's go," orders Jax, shoving Rey and me forward before taking the lead. With the uncomfortable reminder these woods are far from safe because the League wants us dead, I swallow my shock at the night's events and tromp through the underbrush of ferns and shrubs behind Jax with Rey in tow.

Our weapons are drawn, senses alert and every time I hear the smallest sound, I flip toward it convinced the League has snuck upon us again. In their black uniforms and military-style training, a surprise ambush is more than likely. Hair prickles the back of my neck and I'm convinced Elijah lurks behind every tree or thick bush. I can almost feel his eyes boring into my skull and picture his lips twisted in their wicked grin.

A mile behind us, the fire rages as it consumes the League's mall. Smoke and soot float in the breeze, descending upon us like black snow. The smell following long after the forest blocks the scene from view.

We don't speak, too busy listening for sounds of an attack, but I can see tension in Jax's body, his shoulders bunched and neck stiff. I don't think it has to do with fear of running into the League.

Casting occasional glances at Rey behind me, making sure he hasn't dissolved into nothingness, I notice he walks different now too. His lanky gate has become more confident and fluid instead of clumsy like before. In a way, he almost moves like Jax. They both slip through the trees and step across the pine needled, leaf covered earth with a beautiful, soundless grace, a talent I have far from mastered. I cringe each time I crunch on dead leaves or send a pebble scuttling along the ground.

And as we walk, I still can't move past my disbelief at Rey's appearance. I don't understand how any of this can possibly be real. I have a million questions and I want to touch him again and wrap him in my arms and prove to myself this isn't some bizarre dream.

I don't though. We need to survive this night first and make it to safety or it won't matter that Rey has been resurrected from the dead.

CHAPTER TWO

With the pinkish hint of morning sunlight in the sky and the last bit of energy I've managed to muster, we finally push through some full evergreens and find ourselves standing before six ancient brick buildings with white columns, tall paneled doors and rows of wooden paned windows. Most of the buildings are uninhabitable, with roofs caved in and walls nothing more than crumpled piles of brick and rusted iron framework, but to our far right I catch a view of several compound members keeping guard outside two intact structures, the largest of the six, each with three stories and tall, sloping roofs. In some of the windows that aren't boarded up, lanterns and candles flicker like beacons welcoming us to our new home.

Exhausted, we lower our weapons and march toward the guards. I exhale a long breath I didn't even know I'd been holding, tightness releasing from my neck and shoulders. I've made it; survived the League yet again thanks to a combination of Charlie's compound and more luck than I can probably comprehend. Relief floods through me and it's all I can do to not collapse on the grass from sheer exhaustion.

As we approach the nearest of the two buildings, one off the guards, Ivan if I remember correctly, nods his chin to Jax. "Were you followed?"

Jax shakes his head, black hair flopping. "No. We killed four, possibly a fifth, a few miles back and haven't seen any sign of anyone else. I think the aftermath of the fireworks have them a little busy."

The second guard turns toward us and I stiffen, halting in

my tracks so suddenly that Rey smacks into me with an "oof".

From the top step or the main entrance, Raoul's dark, haughty glare drives into me, piercing through my skin like a knife as he sneers. "Looks like the Sub survived after all."

"Shut up, Raoul," growls Jax, shouldering his weapon and nose wrinkling in disgust. "Unless you want a broken cheekbone to match your nose."

"Who's that?" Ivan asks, eyes filled with suspicion while he gestures to Rey.

"Rey Zuritsky," he replies, stepping around me. A second later I realize what I've done and my stomach clenches and knots.

Jax's head jerks around, features twisted as he pieces information together. "Zuritsky? That's the fake last name you gave Daniel and me the night we found you."

Rey turns to me, stunned. "What?"

"I- uh- it's not... I didn't." I trip over three dozen words that seem to be competing for space in my mouth, all trying to escape first. My cheeks redden and palms sweat while I bounce from foot to foot.

"Hold on, we have another Sub?" Raoul demands, probably the only time I'm grateful he opened his stupid mouth. But his face contorts and his right hand constricts on his gun as he stalks down the steps, closer Rey. "How many more are you going to bring here? Don't you see all the trouble they cause? That Sub you keep running off to save is the reason our entire home was burned to the ground!"

"That *Sub*, is the reason your daughter is alive, or did you forget being too coward to save her?"

"What did you just say to me, Cole?" snaps Raoul, left hand balled into a tight fist.

Jax's shoulders lift, muscles bulking as he takes several menacing steps forward until he and Raoul stand toe to toe. His lips curl back in a menacing snarl, reminding me of Tisis. "I said shut your mouth unless you want a broken face again."

"With a mangled hand? I'd like to see you try."

"What? You think I can't kick your ass one-handed? I've already done it once."

Raoul gnashes his teeth, eyes narrowing into two dark slits. "Do it Cole, and I swear to God it will be the last thing you do. I have watched people die, our people, because you and Charlie and a bunch of other idiots around here think these Subs deserve to be saved. They are garbage, worse than the League even! They don't belong here, half the compounds knows it, and if you don't have the guts to shoot them, then I will."

Raoul lifts his weapon, leveling it at my chest and I don't even have a chance to grab mine from my waistband before I become a target once again. I don't need my gun though, because I hear a series of clicks as Jax and Rey both whip theirs forward and flip off the safeties. Ivan jerks his own gun up as well though he waivers uneasily between Raoul and Jax, unsure what to do since both are his friends.

And this is how we stand for several long, apprehensive seconds; Raoul aiming at me, Jax and Rey aiming at him and poor Ivan at a loss of who to aim at while I quiver in the middle, hands raised and mouth parted in fear.

I should be used to having weapons trained on me by now, it seems to happen every other day or so. Sometimes twice a day if I've pissed off enough people, but it terrifies me every time because eventually one time will be my last. An ironic fate considering I always assumed the Gamble would kill me.

However, all I can think as I stare down the steel barrel, is that at what point will people on this planet stop aiming guns at me? I'm one very small girl who didn't even mean to cause half the problems now plaguing us.

"What is going on out here?" a loud, baritone voice booms, causing me to jump as I whip my head toward the entrance of the building. Taking up the entire front door stands a tall, broad man, his shoulders nearly touching each doorframe and his form blocking out whatever dim light comes from inside.

Even though they look nothing alike because this man has dark hair lined with only the first hints of grey, jet black eyes and olive- golden skin, I am reminded of my father. They both stand the same way; powerful and strong and imposing, chin held high and with a gaze so laser- piercing that seems to go straight through the object of their focus, which at this moment appears to be me.

Stomping down the steps he marches across the grass, his heavy boots thumping the earth. As the man strides toward us, behind him I glimpse Charlie, Randolph and Evy, all with the same expressions of horror at the situation before them. Charlie hurries forward, marching after the towering, dark-haired man.

"Lower the weapons!" the man commands, his voice slicing through the air like a bullet of its own.

No one moves.

Raoul's eyes flash, Jax clenches his jaw and I don't think Rey has blinked once in the last minute. The only one that partially follows directions is Ivan, but when no one else does the same, he pauses with his gun half angled at the ground and glances sideways at Charlie, pleading for some sort of guidance.

"Now!" the man roars from deep in his chest. Even furious, he still remains composed, which is almost more frightening than if he let his fury free.

All four men lower their guns, pointing them to the

ground though none flick the safeties back into place and the tension over our little group has only intensified to the level of suffocation.

"Now, who exactly are you?" the man asks, turning his attention back to me where I stand with my hands still stuck in the air. His gaze floats over my face, examining me from head to toe and it feels like my veins have iced over. If I could melt into the dirt and disappear, I would happily do so.

"Kelsey. Kelsey Keslin," I stammer, keeping my arms up in case he decides he wants to aim a gun at me too. Everyone else has, so what's one more?

Head tilting, he regards me with interest, his lips turned into the slightest allusion of an amused smile, accentuating two dimples and the clef of his chin. "Escaped the League twice now, in addition to ROC, if rumors are correct. Word on the street is you survived a gunshot too. You're the young lady that seems to have caused a considerable amount of commotion around here."

"That seems to be the short version," I grumble, relaxing enough to allow my arms to return to my sides. The man's jaw constricts and he continues to stare around at our group. I subconsciously shift closer to Jax, he's saved me twice before after all, and besides, he stands the closest.

Then this coal-haired, stately man bursts into hearty, full-blown laughter, eyes crinkling at the corners. "Then who's the gangly blond kid?"

"My best friend Rey," I say. "He's from the O.Z. too."

"So now you guys are multiplying?"

"How did he get up here?" Charlie asks in bewilderment, moving forward until she stops beside the man.

I'm short. Which means that by my standards, nearly everyone else is tall, including Charlie, but even though she stands with her shoulders squared back and her chin lifted, he dwarfs her by comparison, both in height and shear mass.

Casting a hurried glance at Rey, making sure for the millionth time he hasn't vanished like some figment of my imagination, I lick my lips and swallow the lump that's been sitting in my throat for hours. "I don't know. He... I... I thought he was dead."

"Zombie, huh? Well, come inside, let's get you settled in" the man says, motioning me toward the closest building's front door. "It sounds like you and Rey have a lot to discuss." Then, with his face stern and gaze as sharp as a knife, he turns to Jax, Rey, Raoul and poor Ivan, who still appears baffled and alarmed. "As for the rest of you. This is my compound, therefore my rules. I highly doubt Charlie allows you all to point loaded weapons at each other, but just in case, if I see any of you do it here again, you'll start losing toes or fingernails or whatever is easiest that still allows you to be useful. I don't have the time nor the patience for this nonsense. Am I clear?"

Everyone nods, eyes wide; even Raoul though I can see it pains him to bite his tongue; as they hostler or shoulder their respective guns. Jax, Rey and I scurry through the doorway behind the man, Randolph and Evy trailing as we hear Charlie reprimand Raoul. If I had a choice, I like to see him lose his tongue instead of a few fingernails.

Evy grabs my hand, giving it a gentle squeeze and pulling my attention away from all the men. "Kelsey, I'm so relieved you're ok. What happened? How did-"

"Kelsey, Rey," the man says, interrupting. "I imagine you'd both like some time to speak privately. That door there is an old office, no one will bother you." He indicates a wooden door hanging on a slight angle due to rusty, bent hinges. The words *Resident Advisor* are painted in faded gold letters across the top panel. "Randolph and Evy, you both should get some rest as I understand you're on scheduled to help in the fields later this afternoon. Jaxon, let's go see someone about your hand. That looks like a lot of blood."

"It's not that bad," Jax argues, shifting closer to me.

Nole places a firm hand on his shoulder, steering him to the nearest hallway. "Doesn't matter. It needs to be looked at. Battle scars impress the ladies, gangrenous infections do not."

As he's guided away, Jax twists to stare at me. He wears a mixed expression of concern and puzzlement and a little bit of fearfulness. Probably the first time I've ever seen him actually look worried.

I duck my head to avoid his gaze and feel my heart sink in my chest. With Rey back, however it has somehow come about, my entire world is about to be flung upside down again. This time it will toss Jax into the turmoil as well.

"Who is that guy?" Rey asks as Jax and the man vanish around a bend in the hall.

"Nole Santiago," Randolph replies. "He's the leader of the Risers."

I lift my eyebrows. "Risers?"

"It's what the group here calls themselves. They rise over their obstacles or something like that. They helped us attack the League. Nole's had enough of being terrorized by them too and after our compound was destroyed, he invited us here. I think he's got a thing for Charlie."

"You've got a thing for Charlie," Evy jokes, poking her older brother in the ribs.

He scrunches his face. "Charlie is like twice our age."

"And still pretty darn attractive. Hope I look like her when I'm that old."

"And how old do you think that is, Miss Chung?" asks someone behind us. We spin around to find Charlie entering the building, a slight smile drawn across her lips.

Evy's golden skin transforms into twelve shades of crimson. "Uh... I..."

"Don't you two need to get some sleep? You've had a very long night." Charlie says with an arched eyebrow. "And Kelsey and her friend need some time alone."

Randolph and Evy, heads down and bickering in hushed tones, scamper off into the depths of the complex. Charlie chuckles softly to herself and shakes her head before facing Rey and me again. Reaching out, she smooths my hair and rubs my upper arm.

"Kelsey, I'm glad you're alright. There will be a tiny little girl very happy to see you once you and Rey have had a chance to talk. She and Jax are on the third floor in the old dormitories, suite 307. And Rey, I don't know where you've been living since you got to the surface, but you are welcome to stay here as long as you want. There's plenty of space and as long as you can pull your own weight, Nole and I are happy to have you, whatever some of our people might lead you to believe."

With a last pat on my shoulder, she glides down the hall turning away at a stairwell, until I am alone with Rey. A moment I had fully believed I would never have again.

CHAPTER THREE

"Kels," he whispers, drawing me into a firm embrace until there's no more space between us; like we are two magnets that have fought so painfully hard to be together again. Now everything is right in the world.

I close my eyes and rest my cheek against his chest. I hear his heartbeat, steady and calm. It brings back memories of our last night together, when all I wanted to do was lie with him and listen to this beautiful sound that was doomed to never sing again. Even though his eyes look different and his walk is different, his heartbeat has stayed exactly the same.

If he is somehow a ghost, somehow not actually here and maybe this really is all a crazy illusion by my mind driven mad, I don't care. I could still be imprisoned in the League's basement, Rey a hallucination from the drugs they gave me to keep me compliant, and I'd be perfectly happy with that if it means Rey never leaves again. He feels real, he smells like Rey and as I wrap my arms tighter around him and he kisses the top of my head, joy wells inside me, erasing all the horrible, excruciating memories of the last few weeks. If this is insanity, then I never want to be sane again.

We stand in the hall for nearly five minutes, locked in each other's arms, neither wanting to be the first to end these blissful moments. I cling to him, afraid that if I let go he might fade away like fragments of a wonderful dream. I never want to let go. Unless someone pries us apart, I might stay like this forever because I'm finally home again. Not home where I was trapped underground or a prisoner to the Gamble, but home where I was safe and comfortable with no one pointing guns at my head and where Rey always stood beside me, ready to take on the world, even if we had no idea how big the world really was. We had no idea of anything, and right now, that doesn't matter at all.

Cupping my chin in his hands, Rey draws my face to his and kisses me, tender and soft, his thumbs stroking my cheeks. I melt against him, forgetting everything else that has happened, doing all I can to savor the moment. He tastes of fresh air and sunshine.

As we pull apart, I gaze into his eyes. "Rey, I don't understand. How are you here? I saw you go into the chambers. No one ever comes back out. You... you were dead."

"Come on," he says, taking my hand, entwining his long fingers with mine before leading me into the old office. His soft touch sends tingles radiating through my body.

Entering the space, I gaze around at the cluttered room filled with the last remnants and traces of someone long gone. Whether its previous owner survived the bombs or not, they have been dead a while and it's strange to think that way. That the person probably came here nearly every day for years, organized the room, worked in here and laughed in here and lived so much of their life in here, and then one day raced out in a horrified panic to never return again.

On one side sits a battered desk, supported mostly by large rocks since three legs have been snapped off, possibly for firewood at some point. Four mismatched chairs of varying styles circle around it like short stocky guards. Metal bookshelves line the far wall, most of the paper volumes turned nearly to dust over the past century though several plastic binders have remained intact, their edges warped and brittle and the documents inside undoubtedly unrecognizable.

An ancient, dusty computer with a logo of three-quarters of an apple on its back panel rests on the floor in the far corner, inoperable and obsolete in a world that no longer offers electricity and with people who probably have no idea how to use a computer should power grids ever be restored. It occurs to me that Rey and I are perhaps the only people on the surface of the world who would know how to use it if it were operable. I wonder what sort of information hides on that hard-drive, never to be seen again. So many things that had once been important, relegated to useless dust and garbage when the world fell to pieces.

A row of grubby windows overlooks the forest. Rey leads me to them where we perch on the wide wooden ledge and watch the sun start its daily journey across the sky, its bright gleam scattering the darkness.

"I escaped," he says eventually, staring through the grime on the glass and into the picturesque world beyond, his face reflects back so I stare at two of him instead of one.

"But how?"

Turning back toward me, I realize his eyes are the exact shade of blue as the sky, his hair the color of the rays of the morning sun, his once pale skin now tan and glowing with a small smattering of freckles across his nose. He looks healthier, happier, more like Rey than he ever did inside ROC. He belongs up here on the surface, he always has.

"The air ducts," he replies, brushing a hand through his hair, the locks falling past his shoulders. "When I first started working last year, I found some really old blueprints of the O.Z. My supervisor told me they were useless and mostly wrong, which they were, but I was curious and studied them anyway because they were interesting, you know how I am about that kind of stuff. Anyway, the blueprints indicated a vent in the chambers, and a shaft that seemed to lead above ground, which made sense because the poisonous gas has to ventilate somewhere. Or at least at one point it must have ventilated through there, I don't know. I didn't really think much of it until my number was called. Then, that night while I watched you sleep, a plan formed in my head. It seemed crazy, but what choice did I have? I had a hand drill in my pocket, you know the one that's really small that I always carry? Once they locked the chamber doors, I unscrewed and wrenched the grate off the vent and started to climb."

My eyes widen in astonishment. "And no one stopped you?"

"Well, it's not like Gendarme hang out in the chambers. Besides, there were several thousand people crammed in there. We barely had enough room to breathe let alone see more than a foot in front of us. Most of the people didn't notice, and those in the chambers who did thought I was nuts and just going to die anyway. Maybe I was but I didn't care anymore. I'd rather die fighting than cowering like everyone else, crying and moaning for their families. At least, in whatever time I had left, I could say I tried."

"You've always been a fighter," I whisper.

Laughing to himself, he sits back against the splintered frame of the window, bringing one knee to his chest and resting an elbow on it. "The first four hundred feet were the hardest because I had to brace myself against opposite walls with my feet and my back and climb straight up. If I weren't so strong from all that equipment I hauled every day, and used to being cramped inside the ducts from work, I'd have never made it. After that though it got easy, the shaft mostly leveled out to a reasonable incline and I crawled for hours through the twists and turns and upward slops until I finally reached the exit above ground. It was dark by the time I got out."

"Where have you been since?" I ask, unable to fathom that Rey and I both escaped ROC within a few hours of each other, probably even less than a mile from each other, and had no idea.

"I've been lying low the last few weeks, living in old buildings and stuff, hunting for small animals, stealing from random vegetable fields and orchards if I was certain I wouldn't get caught. I stayed away from any people, mostly because I was so shocked there were people, you know?"

Now it's my turn to laugh. "Yeah, I was a little surprised too."

"Oh, I can picture the look on your face," he says, grinning. "Anyway, I saw the giant fire last night and got curious. I'd seen the League before, from a distance. With their machine guns and black armor they looked like the Gendarme and I figured anything that looked like the Gendarme probably wasn't good so I kept away. While I was wandering through the woods last night toward the fire, I heard that guy, Jax, yelling your name. I thought it was too good to be true, that it must have been someone else with the same name because you'd never be up here and yet..."

"And yet I escaped too." Chewing on my bottom lip, I process what he's said, how brave he was and what he's been through to survive. He's had no help, no knowledge of the surface, and managed to stay alive and out of trouble. Meanwhile, I've started a small war, had Charlie's compound destroyed, murdered several people and nearly died at least twice.

"So, after all that effort to escape the chambers, you weren't thinking about dying from the radiation?" I ask.

"There is no radiation."

"Right, but we didn't know that." I hope he doesn't ask me why I was willing to succumb to the radiation because I'm not ready to share my crazy story just yet, especially the part about wanting to die because I thought he had. I feel foolish because, in looking back with what I know now, the choice seems so dramatic, though I will never forget the crushing pain I felt believing he was gone. I pray I never have to live it again because next time I won't survive. Hindsight might be twenty-twenty, but grief is insurmountable blindness.

Lost in thought, Rey remains quiet for a long time, watching the woods surrounding our building as if it's the first time he's seen trees. I guess it practically is and I wonder if Jax ever sees me staring at them the same way. Or maybe the sky. I know I gawk endlessly at that vast space overhead, still in awe at something everyone else up here takes for granted and most don't even acknowledge except to make comments on the weather.

"I did know there wasn't radiation," he says eventually. "At least, I strongly suspected it."

I blink in surprise. "What? How could you?"

"There's a group, Kelsey, a small one in the Subs that believes the surface is habitable and that the Council is lying to us."

"What?"

"They call themselves Guardians of the Truth and they recruited me about a year ago, once I started working. I guess, given my line of work and the fact I had no parents to stop me, I was the perfect candidate. They're the ones that made me believe there was a way out based on the blueprints I found. That's why I climbed through that vent, why I pushed myself forward even when I thought death was easier. I had to know if they were right. They want to fight against the Councilmembers and the Gendarme; if they ever manage to gather enough people willing to do so; and they want to live on the surface again."

"Rey, I don't understand. How could anyone possibly know? It's been a century, anyone who could have known has been dead for decades, and that's assuming the original ROC citizens weren't feed the same lies about bombs and the end of the world that we were. I can't imagine the Councilmembers are going around telling anyone the truth, I doubt their own families even know."

Once again Rey runs his hands through his tangled, knotted hair, something he always does when a difficult topic arises. "I'm not sure. Right now, all they have are guesses and suspicions and with the Council watching every citizen's movements through those cameras and whatnot, it's hard to talk about it, or to get more people on board. One of them, Jericho, the man who got me involved, was the partially blind man with that old woman you met our last night in ROC. He's one of the leaders."

I think back to that night, how the terrified man tried to shove the door shut in my face. When the Protector's own daughter showed up at his suite, he must have thought he'd been found out and that his family was in danger.

Plotting against the Council, even if the Council has no tangible proof of a plot; not that they need it; it's completely insane. Anyone caught would have their number in the Gamble so many times they'd never survive, provided they weren't immediately executed for treason or terrorism or whatever other charges the Council and the Gendarme prosecuted them for. Even their family's numbers could be added to the Gamble too for additional punishment or inclusion in a crime. The possibilities are endless because the Council would never stand for any sort of rebelliousness. Neither would the other citizens if they thought their own safety were at risk if ROC were destroyed.

Were there really people willing to do this, to stand against the Council, even with almost no tangible evidence of their suspicions? How could they have any idea the Unoccupied Zone is actually, in fact, occupied? How could they recruit people with theories so radical, I'm still not sure I believe it, and I've been *living* it?

Then another jarring thought occurs and I feel the start of hot anger boiling in my gut. "You were involved in all this, and you never told me?"

"Kelsey, your father is the Protector."

"So?"

"Are you kidding? What do you think would happen if he found out?"

"But I wouldn't have told him! I'd never betray you! Look at the other things we've done that could have gotten us punished and I never said a word."

"That's not the same and that's not why I didn't tell you."

"Then why not? What did you think I would have done? Told Wyatt?"

"You wouldn't have believed me!" Rey exclaims, throwing his arms wide, smacking the window with one hand. "I barely believed it. No one had any way to prove it. It's not like we could go waltzing out the door onto the surface to check things out."

"But you didn't even give me a chance?" I demand, shoving up from my seat, hurt and livid that Rey, my best friend, didn't trust me with the biggest secret of his life, something that could have changed the future for both of us. "After all the years we've known each other, after I agreed to *marry* you, you honestly thought I'd accuse you of lying, or worse, betray you to my father?"

"I didn't want you involved! It was too dangerous. What we were doing, what we believed and what we were planning, we all could have died because of it. I couldn't put you in that kind of danger. I'd never risk your life like that."

"So you left me behind," I say coolly, arms folded over my chest as burning tears form behind my eyes. "You knew all of this, knew there was a chance we could survive up here and yet you said nothing, not even on our last night together when I wanted to run away."

"I tried to tell you on your birthday. When we were sitting on the bench and you were so upset about your arranged marriage, remember? I told you there was a way out of all of that. I just, I couldn't bring myself to tell you everything."

"Don't even try to act like you told me anything. I had no idea what that statement meant and you knew it! And then you went in the chambers and left me behind to believe you were dead. Do you realize what you've done to me, Rey? How badly that hurt? What I went through?"

He lunges to his feet, hands balled into fists. His cheeks are flushed and splotchy, the way they always are when he's upset. "And you think that wasn't killing me? You think I was happy knowing I'd never see you again? I didn't know what was up here, if I'd make it or if we were wrong about the radiation or if I'd get caught and shot. I left you behind because you were safe. That's all I ever wanted for you!"

"Safe? SAFE!" I shriek, slamming a hand against the ledge of the window and causing the panes to rattle. Tiny splinters dig into my palm but the sting of pain pales to the rage blistering inside my chest and I think I might explode. "The Gamble, the Gendarme, the rations, having to marry Wyatt freaking Walker. You think all of that meant I was safe?"

"Yes! It did! Maybe not happy, but you'd be safe. The odds of your number ever being called-"

"No! No, I was a prisoner Rey, just like you and everyone else in the O.Z, living in constant fear of running out of resources or breaking one of the thousands of laws or having my number selected in the Gamble. And you left me there to face whatever pathetic future ROC held in those suffocating grey walls. I could have died down there just as easily as up here. Do you even know why I'm up here in the first place? Why I left ROC? It's because you died and I wanted to die too. I couldn't imagine a world without you in it so I came to the surface hoping the radiation would kill me."

His face tumbles into an expression of stunned sorrow. He opens and closes his mouth several times before finding words. "Kels, I didn't... I didn't think..."

He reaches for me but I slap his arms away. Tears cascade down my cheeks, scorching my skin. "No, you didn't. You didn't even think to give me a chance, did you? I would have gone with you in a heartbeat if you had asked, if you had actually said anything at all. Even if it meant we would die, I'd have rather died with you than spend the rest of my life without!"

I shove past him and storm from the room, almost stumbling over my own feet because I am so blinded by my roaring emotions and the wave of tears.

Rey doesn't follow.

CHAPTER FOUR

It takes me several minutes to regain any sort of composure and dry my eyes, swollen and red from tears and anger and insurmountable exhaustion, a weariness so deep in my bones I don't know if it can ever be cured.

I sit in a vacant stairwell of concrete and metal, forcing myself to find a sense of calm before I go in search of Jax's suite. He's already distrusting of Rey, I don't want to have to explain why I'm crying and that my best friend didn't share a secret that would have changed the entire world we knew. Could have changed everything that has happened in the last few weeks.

As I take a final shuddering breath, I press to my feet and ascend to the third floor. It's weird on the surface that the floors go up with the numbers so that higher numbered floors are on the top, closer to the sky. In ROC it was the opposite with higher numbered sectors further into the earth. However, despite the difference in numbering, the poorly lit and somberly decorated halls and stairs and sectioned off living quarters of the former dormitory remind me of ROC. I grimace at the thought of being back underground in that stifling monotony. I need windows and sunlight and fresh air. Now that I have tasted true freedom, the idea of ROC terrifies me even more, being sealed inside that underground tomb.

At the far end of the third floor, I locate suite 307, though the 7 hangs upside down by one screw and the rest of the plastic, painted numbers are chipped and cracked. I debate knocking on the hollow aluminum door, warped and dented from age, but technically this is my new home too so, after finding it unlocked, I slip into the tiny living quarters. At least on the surface I don't have to scan my barcode.

The dormitory common room lies empty with the exception of a sagging, faded sofa and chair by the far windows. A small kitchenette branches off on one side with a rusted sink and a fridge missing its door and interior shelves, not that the unit works anyway in a world devoid of electricity.

The peeling walls had probably once been white, but are now discolored and cracked, the sheetrock deteriorating from the bottom up. In some places I can glimpse metal supports and wooden framing. The stained and marred wood floor creaks and strains under my footsteps and some floorboards look like they've been recently replaced to remove rotting pieces of wood.

As I look for windows, something I've become so accustomed to doing lately, I see one has been covered with plywood, its glass shattered and gone.

Branching off to my right, a short hallway leads to three small bedrooms and a bathroom with just a shower stall. I wondered who lived here once, in these buildings that had been a boarding school before the world changed forever.

At the sound of my approach, Jax slips from one of the bedrooms, pulling the door ajar behind him with a slight squeak in its hinges. At first neither of us move toward each other, instead standing at opposite ends of the hall, staring like two soldiers on opposing sides of a battlefield. He looks exhausted, but there's more... a wary awkwardness, like he is unsure of how to handle me, such a drastic change from the confident, arrogant boy willing to shoot me a month ago.

Jax isn't an idiot. I wonder if he's pieced together my history with Rey, that we once, however briefly, were more than friends. That I'm in love with Rey and that now he is back and here with us, things will become so much more complicated. As if our lives aren't already complex enough.

I don't know what to think or how to feel or what I even want, and right now I am too tired and sore and beaten to try, so I take several steps toward Jax, curious to see how he will react. Will he move closer or shift away?

He does neither, instead standing a little straighter, shoulders squared and chin lifted higher. It's the posture of someone who wants to appear strong and self-assured, which he is, but someone who also recognizes they are about to have that strength and assurance tested in the worst way. It's the façade of someone who sees a battle coming, and knows they have a fifty-fifty chance either way.

"How's your hand?" I ask.

With a glance at the clean linen winding his fingers, he shrugs. "Just flesh wounds. Someone stitched the bad ones, said I should be able to take the bandages off in a couple days."

"Does it hurt bad?"

"No."

I'm sure he's lying, there's no way an injury like that wouldn't hurt, but Jax won't admit pain or weakness, not even to himself.

"How's Nadia?" I whisper, nodding toward the door behind him.

"She's fine, just fell asleep. Tisis is with her. Apparently she's been up all night waiting for us."

Shaking my head, I laugh softly. "She would be. Sometimes I forget she's eight, she acts so much older. I'm going to see her."

Slipping by Jax in the narrow hall, our shoulders brush and with his good hand he reaches out to grasp my upper arm, his fingers hot against my skin. I turn to meet his gorgeous eyes that seem to make my heart skip a beat every time and I suddenly know that whatever the near future holds, it's going to be far more than just complicated.

"Are you ok?" he asks.

I hang my head. I wonder if he can see the redness in my eyes from the tears. "You always ask me that, Jax and I'm always fine."

"Even with your friend?"

I purse my lips and continue to look at the floor. A deep gouge is carved into the wooden slates, as though something extremely heavy was dropped long ago. Without thinking, I run the toe of my boot in it.

"His name is Rey," I say, fighting my emotions back into the recesses of my mind. "And I honestly don't know. It's... a lot to take in and some of what he told me, about how he got up here, just... it makes me question even more than I was already questioning. Whatever was happening in ROC, it's beyond anything I could imagine. Every time I think I've finally sorted through the lies, I find myself trapped in a dozen more."

"But you don't have to worry about ROC anymore."

"I'll always worry about ROC. It's a part of who I am. Being on the surface, regardless of what happens here, that will never change. We can't erase our past just because our future took a different course."

Instantly, Jax's entire demeanor changes, body relaxing as he moves closer until we're barely a few inches apart. In the comfort of his presence, I relax too, leaning against the wall and closing my eyes as he places his bandaged hand on the wall beside my head. Then he brushes his other hand through my hair. My curls are so gross and dirty and caked with dried blood and pine needles and who even knows, I don't know why he wants to touch them, but his fingers are gentle and he rests his palm on the side of my neck running a thumb across the line of my jaw.

"I know," he says. "You're right."

"Jax," I murmur, opening my eyes again. "What did you try to tell me last night? When we were watching the fireworks?"

He smiles, but it is sad and vacant, the same expression he wore the one time he talked about his family. "It doesn't really matter now."

I nod. I think I know what he was going to say, but I'm not ready to hear it and certainly not ready to acknowledge it. I need more time, so instead of saying anything, I press up from the wall and duck around him.

"I should get some sleep. It's been a rough few days."

"Ok," he says. "There's an empty bed in the first bedroom. One of the Risers brought up clean blankets earlier so it's all ready for you.

"Where will you sleep? The third bedroom?"

He moves toward the main room of the apartment. "The third room is empty, there's no furniture. I'll take the couch in the living room."

Watching his retreating form, I feel myself grow cold and lonely the farther he travels from me. It wraps around me like an icy, rough blanket and I can't seem to make it go away.

"Jax," I call. He turns, eyebrows lifted and expression curious as I pause, chewing on my lip. What I'm about to say, what I'm about to ask for, I know I shouldn't. I know that our lives are about to become so much more difficult and uncertain and that most of the difficulty will be because of me, because of choices I'll have to make.

But I am selfish and don't want to think about that today. I know it's not fair, not when Rey is here and I just kissed him twenty minutes ago and I haven't been remotely honest with either of them about the other. Right now though, I am so scared and lost inside, I need Jax. I need to forget about the last few hours and all of the reminders of ROC that Rey's arrival has stirred up. I know that deep down, on some sub-level neither of us wants to investigate, Jax understands me. He always will. Tattoos and demons.

"You don't have to sleep on the couch," I say. "I mean, if you don't want to."

His head lifts at an angle, and I can feel the energy between us again, pulsing and alive.

"What do you want?" he asks carefully.

I don't know. I don't know what I want anymore it's all such a mess. I want to go back to April fourteenth, before the Gamble, before I knew my father arranged for me to marry Wyatt, before I left ROC and started a war. Back when it was just Rey and me and a delicate little sugar cookie.

I can't go back though, and even if I could, it would mean eradicating Jax from my life and just like with Rey, I can't imagine a world without him.

I bite the inside of my mouth and take a deep breathe. "I want to feel safe. Can you stay with me? Just for a little bit."

For a moment I think he's going to refuse and I might burst into tears if he does, my emotions so fragile and raw from the stress of everything.

But then he walks back to me until we're mere inches from each other and I can hear him breathing, the only sound in the quiet space save the steady pound of my heart, quickening as he nears.

He touches me again, smoothing my hair aside. "Why don't you get cleaned up first. There's clean water in the bathroom and several changes of clothes for us."

Nodding, I turn away into the bathroom and shut the door, leaning against it for a moment.

A large bucket of water sits in the old, stained shower base. A mirror hangs over the vanity, its glass cracked down the center and separating my reflection into two halves. Neither half looks all that great; skin a mottled mess of cuts and bruises, a busted lip, hair flying every direction.

Stripping naked, I clean the grime and blood and dried sweat from my body, rinse my hair for all the good it will do and scrub away the dirt caked under my ragged, broken fingernails.

A pair of faded black shorts and a pink tank top with one strap hanging by a few threads sit in a pile on the floor. They're a little too big, but as I look in the mirror again and see how much weight I've lost from my already tiny frame, I guess most clothes will be too big now. I've lost the few womanly curves I'd started to form, looking more like my thirteen-year-old self than a young adult.

I at least feel human again as I wander back to the bedroom, the room dim with the worn curtains pulled across the single window to block out the morning sunlight. Jax lies on the bed, arms latched behind his head with the blanket pulled up to his waist, leaving his muscular chest bare and exposed. My heart beats faster.

His eyes are closed and I think he's already asleep, but as I step into the room, he opens them and sits up, staring at me with a guarded hope, as afraid of rejection as I am.

Suddenly I'm nervous but I don't know why. It's not like anything is going to happen, and it's not like I've never slept next to a guy before because there was that one night with Rey. But maybe I'm nervous because Rey is downstairs. Or maybe I'm nervous because it's Jax and there's something between us I don't fully understand yet, a sharp vulnerability I've never felt before, something I know I can get hurt on.

"Kelsey, I can sleep on the couch," he says, rising from the bed and crossing the room. "Really, it's fine."

But as he moves closer, my apprehension melts away. "No, please. I want you here."

I pad across the moth-eaten carpet and slide between the cool, patched sheets. After a moment, Jax slips in beside me, drawing me into his arms until my face presses against his chest. I feel secure and protected, forgetting that less than twelve hours ago I lied in a dark cell waiting for my death.

"We didn't destroy the League completely, did we?" I ask softly.

His fingers twist through my damp hair, lightly pulling at the loose curls. "No."

"And Sawyer and Elijah are still alive?"

"Probably."

"Which means we aren't done with them yet."

Moving slightly, Jax pulls away until our heads rest on separate pillows and we gaze at each other. He still wears the scar on his forehead that Elijah gave him when I let myself be taken. Seeing it again makes me feel sick because Jax was hurt because of me.

"Nole and Charlie have a plan," he says. "I don't know the details, I was more focused on rescuing you, but they are done being terrorized by the League. It's time the League was terrorized by us."

"Even with the Risers on our side, and with the damage we did to the League, they still outnumber us."

Jax pulls the blanket up to my shoulders, tucking it around me and then slipping an arm under my neck so that I am partially supported by his body, warm and hard beside me.

"Kelsey, after what you have been through, right now you

only need to worry about sleeping."

"I won't feel safe until they're dead."

"You're safe with me. Always."

Then he kisses me delicately and caresses my back. I allow myself to unwind and slip into the first comforts of sleep.

But my last thought, is that tomorrow I have so very many things to worry about.

* * *

I'm awoken hours later by a noise, a soft click I wouldn't normally notice, but in the quiet apartment, with my senses already on heightened alert, it might as well have been one of Jax's fireworks.

Launching up, I realize I am alone, Jax has vanished, leaving the bed frigid and igniting my frazzled nerves. I shiver despite the room being humid and muggy from the mid-spring air outside. Glancing out the window, I see darkness creep past the curtain. I must have slept the entire day.

"Hello? Jax? Nadia?"

My calls are met only with silence. It's not, however, the soothing kind. It's the heavy, ominous kind that sets the tiny hairs along my arms on edge. As silent as the air around me, I slither from the bed. I have no idea where my gun has been put and I'm kicking myself for yet again being unarmed. Jax keeps one nearby, but he is gone, and I am weaponless.

In the pressing darkness, I tiptoe to the edge of the doorframe, peering into the hallway and trying to see the main door. Light from the moon outside flitters through the common room windows, casting everything in an unearthly grey glow.

A tall shadow unfurls in the light. One that doesn't belong to Jax and certainly not to Nadia.

My heart rate accelerates as I glance around for anything I

can use to defend myself and find nothing. A floorboard creaks, one at the end of the hall and I realize I have about twenty seconds to figure out where to go before I am seen.

Allowing the darkness to close around me, I retreat into the bedroom. Knowing I can't scale a three-story building, my only option is the wide closet, so I sneak inside and crack the folding door just a sliver. I'm shaking, my hands shivering with fear and palms sweaty.

The figure appears in the bedroom doorway; a man; his form taking up nearly the entire space. My breath constricts in my throat and I draw my hands to my mouth to stifle any cries that might try to escape. My heart thunders so loud, surely it will betray me.

The man steps into the room and I see the outline of a gun in his hand. A million possibilities and potential scenarios race through my brain, each worse than the last. And all I can think is that I'm stupid enough to yet again be caught without so much as a butter knife.

I scoot myself into the farthest corner of the confined space for whatever good it will do. Muffled footsteps fall on the bedroom carpet and I know the man stands directly outside the closet, less than a foot from my hiding spot. Shrinking against the back wall, flattening myself into the cool plaster, I silently pray to whatever gods might be listening to please let me survive, just once more.

But perhaps they have decided I have already had enough chances. Through the slit in the door, I see the man reach forward and clasp the knob, slowly opening the door outward until we are face to face and I can hide no longer.

"Hello, Kelsey," Elijah whispers. "Sawyer and I weren't done with you yet."

I open my mouth and scream.

CHAPTER FIVE

Lashing out with both hands, I lunge forward even though I will never be a match for his gun. My fists fly and feet thrash as I try to connect with his face or his stomach or anything that will give me a small window in which to flee.

"Kelsey!" he bellows, his breath brushing my neck. Except it's not Elijah's voice. Suddenly arms grab me from behind, and I'm pulled tight against someone.

"Stop! Stop, Kelsey, it's me."

Panting and drenched in sweat, my pulse pounding so hard I hear the blood pump in my ears, I flick my eyes across my surroundings. I'm still in the bedroom, but daylight creeps past the curtain, not darkness, marking late afternoon. I'm sitting bolt upright in bed, held tight as I struggle against my captive.

Jerking free, I whip around to find Jax staring, his eyes wide and mouth open in terrified surprise. "You were having a bad dream."

Casting a frantic look around the room again, I realize I am safe. Elijah isn't here. He's never been here. A bad dream, that's all it was.

Folding my knees to my chest, I place my elbows on them before dropping my head into my quivering palms and let out a long exhale to sooth the adrenaline in my veins.

"I'm sorry," I say, my words muffled by my hands as my heart finally begins to slow. "I'm sorry. It was Elijah. He came here for me."

The bed sheets rustle and Jax takes me into his arms, leaning me backward to his chest until his chin rests on my shoulder, lips brushing my cheek in a light kiss. "If Elijah shows his ugly, stupid face here, I'll knock his oversized teeth down his throat."

Despite the fear still running through my blood and the fogginess of my mind trapped in the last vestiges of sleep, I giggle. Twisting around, I face Jax. We're so close, separated by nothing but a hint of empty space. He hasn't let go of me.

His hair lays flat on one side and sticks straight out on the other and it almost makes me laugh again.

"I'm sorry I woke you," I say, trying to tame the wild side of his hair. He catches my hand and kisses the back of it.

"It's ok. Go back to sleep, it's only been a few hours."

Guiding me down onto my pillow, resting my head on his arm, Jax holds me against him. He fits his body to mine as if we are two connecting pieces of a puzzle. Brushing my hair aside, baring my skin, Jax presses his lips to the back of my shoulder just along the top of my shoulder blade. It sends a gentle prickle down my spine.

I'm nearly asleep once more, secure and reassured in his arms, my eyelids tugging shut when a thought occurs to me and I launch myself upright again. "Nadia!"

"Is in the other room asleep," Jax replies, his voice tired, as if he's already fallen back to sleep.

"But she would have heard me scream and come in here, but she didn't!"

I'm out of the bed and in the hall before Jax can even toss the blankets away. Nadia's door yawns wide open and I immediately see that both her and Tisis are gone, the bed unmade and her shoes and nightclothes strewn carelessly on the floor.

"Nadia!" I cry again, hurrying into the vacant common

room. The front door is unlocked and I fling it open, rushing through the hall for the stairs, all while calling her name, not caring who I might disturb. My bare feet slap the concrete stairs, stinging the bottoms as I fly downward in a frenzy.

Reaching the first floor where the old classrooms and offices reside, I bang open the stairwell door, round a corner and smack into Charlie who stumbles backward from the force of impact. Upon seeing the frenetic look across my face, she clutches my upper arms to steady me.

"Kelsey, what's wrong?"

"I can't find Nadia. She's not in the suite." I'm breathless and panicked, convinced something has gone wrong because up here on the surface, nothing is ever the way it should be. Things always go wrong. Maybe my nightmare was a warning. What if Elijah did come and take Nadia? What better way to hurt me?

"She's fine," Charlie says, placing a hand on my shoulder. "I just saw her with Rey."

It takes me a second to process her words as I stare dumbfounded. "With Rey…"

I've forgotten Rey is here, alive again, or never dead in the first place if I want to be technical. It still feels surreal and disorienting. I reach a hand out for the paint-chipped wall to stabilize myself. The stairwell door opens and Jax nearly collides with both of us, shirtless and his hair still disheveled.

Charlie glances between Jax and me, clearly noting his attire, or lack thereof. My face flushes. She raises both eyebrows and puckers her lips. I'm expecting a reprimand but instead she says, "they're outside."

Brushing past her, I stride to the front door, Jax on my heels. Rey and Nadia perch on the top step absorbing the last rays of the day's golden sunshine. An antique, yellowed book with crinkled pages rests open on her lap.

"Con... con-for... con-form," Nadia stammers, over exaggerating the pronunciation before squishing her nose to look up at him hopefully.

"Conform," Rey corrects. "It means to follow laws or rules."

"Like in the O.Z?"

"Exactly like in the O.Z."

"I don't like to conform."

Rey chuckles. "That's fine, there are plenty of times where you don't need to and you should learn to think for yourself. But it's not always a bad thing. The O.Z. has just taken it to an extreme."

I'm reminded of our conversation last night, everything that Rey admitted, all the laws he broke. He's certainly not one to conform.

I'm no longer mad. I could never stay mad at Rey for longer than a few hours, not even when, in a temper tantrum, he accidently broke my favorite doll when we were kids. Now I'm in awe, amazed that he risked so much, had such faith in possibilities no one could prove. While I cried about an arranged marriage, he was helping to plot an entire revolt against the Council and still found time to remember my birthday, steal a cookie, and ease my troubles. He sold his number to the Gamble hundreds of times, to save others from dying and never once asked for anything in return.

"Nadia," I say again, rushing forward to kneel beside her and drawing their attention away from the book. "What are you doing? Where have you been?"

Her big round eyes widen even more as she hops up to hug me, her skinny arms latching around my neck. "Kelsey! Jax told me they got you back. And look, I met Rey. He says he's from the O.Z. and that you're friends. Rey is teaching me how to read since I missed school today."

Untangling myself from her grip, I hold her at arm's length, hands on her boney shoulders, my expression stern. "You can't go off like that. I didn't know where you were."

She stares at me, confused, her previous joy evaporating. "But I didn't go anywhere. I've been here the whole time with Rey, we only barely left the building."

I realize my admonishment is lost on her. For someone who has known nothing but the confines of ROC and then imprisonment with the League, as far as she's concerned, she really didn't go anywhere because she's still at the school building, sitting right outside the front door. She feels safe here. She *is* safe here, with people who will look out for her rather than harm her. She stayed inside the unofficial barricade we've unknowingly assigned. Another confinement for her.

"Ok," I say carefully, not wanting to take the smallest bit of freedom from someone who survived too much to ever be trapped again. "Well, next time if you want to go outside the suite or the building without Jax or me, can you let one of us know? Even if we're asleep. I'll worry otherwise."

"Hey Nadia," Jax calls and I've almost forgotten he's right behind me. "You hungry? Let's go figure out some dinner."

She looks at him while squinting one honey-flecked, dark brown eye against the setting sun. "You don't have a shirt on."

Glancing down, he rubs at his eyes as if he's still fatigued, which, considering the night we endured, is a good possibility. "Right. I'll find a shirt and then we'll get dinner. It smells like someone on dinner crew made fresh bread today. Maybe they have a loaf left over."

Nadia scampers inside, Jax behind her and suddenly I'm alone with Rey, who still sits on the steps, arms on his knees as he watches the sun light the sky with an array of dazzling colors; mauve and cerulean and indigo. I watch it in wonderment as well. I still can't believe how beautiful the sunset is.

Or that Rey is really here.

My emotions have tempered from our fight, grateful instead that my best friend is back, only a few feet away. How many people would give everything they have for a loved one to be returned from death? Having him beside me makes everything else I suffered worth it. I survived a living nightmare, and this is my reward.

Running my hands through my knotted hair, I stroll over and sit on the step next to him so our shoulders almost touch. His skin is tan and glowing, and freckles, ones that I had never noticed before, dot his cheeks and arms.

"Hey," I whisper, nudging his shoulder with my own.

"Hey," he says back, repeating the gesture.

"I'm not apologizing for what I said earlier." I've always loved how I can be straight and to-the-point with Rey. We never waste time on niceties when there's more important things to be said.

He snorts and smiles. "I wouldn't expect you to. You had every right to be upset. I'm not, however, apologizing for not telling you. I did what I thought was right, what would keep you safest. I'd never be able to live with myself if I told you and you got hurt. You know that, right?"

"I know, Rey. It was just a lot to take in on top of everything else."

"It's all been a lot to take in. Half the time I think I'm dreaming and the other half..." He shakes his head and wrinkles his face as if it's too much to contemplate and he can't handle it. Then he shifts slightly until our shoulders prop against each other, as if we are two walls holding up a building. "How did you end up on the surface anyway?"

I sigh, gazing over the tops of the trees to where the bottom edge of the sun hovers over the horizon, bathing in the world in pinkish- blue light. Lightening bugs float up from the grass, dancing through the air as crickets begin their nightly symphony for accompaniment.

"That does seem to be the story of the year. I stole a gun, held Wyatt as hostage and forced him to open the exterior door."

Eyebrows lifting, Rey stares at me, eyes sparkling with a mixture of shock and admiration. "Seriously? Geez, Kels." Then he laughs. "Would have loved to see the look on his face when you pulled a gun on him. You know, the first time I saw you I said to myself, that girl looks like she's gonna be pretty awesome, we should probably be friends. Glad I was right."

Grinning, I feel a bit of pride swell. And for the first time since I stepped a foot out of ROC, I share the full, true story. How, after Rey was gone, I wanted to die. How I found my father's gun and kidnapped Wyatt. How Jax and Daniel stumbled upon and captured me because they thought I was a spy, and how Randolph eventually shot me for trying to escape, prompting Rey to ask to see the permanent scar on my shoulder.

I told him about both experiences with the League, about rescuing Nadia and about the other ROC citizens that had escaped and are now dead because I'd been fool enough to trust Sawyer. I talk about the people I have killed and those I watched die; Daniel and Ashlynn and total strangers; and by the end tears dampen my face. I can taste the salt of them on my lips and a tightness has formed in my chest.

I feel a pressure on my hand as it grips the edge of the stair I sit on. Glancing down I see Rey's long fingers knotted with mine, squeezing for reassurance. Resting my head against his shoulder, he reaches out and holds me tight to his side.

Suddenly it's like nothing has ever changed, as though

the story I just voiced was nothing more than a bad dream or a book I had read. A story that had happened to another person, not to me.

Together we watch the sun dip below the horizon, the sky bruising with the first indigo colors of night. The weather has grown warmer, the air heavy and muggy, but I don't even mind because it feels good against my skin, better than the coldness of the League's basement and certainly better than the weatherless artificial air of ROC set at a constant sixty-six degrees. For energy conservation, even the temperature in the individual suites can't be changed. Whether you're too hot or too cold, you deal with it.

Rey pulls me closer and, with tender fingers on the side of my face, lifts my chin. I know he's going to kiss me and I know I should push him away. I just woke up an hour ago beside Jax. It's not fair to Rey, especially since he doesn't even know.

But I let him kiss me anyway because it's been so long without him and because I'm pretty sure I'm just an awful person and I only care about what I want. Right now, I want both of them because I care about both of them.

Like our first, Rey's kiss is compassionate and slow, giving me plenty of opportunity to draw away if I choose. I don't. Instead, I wind my fingers around his neck as his hands slide into my hair, holding us together. Few a few sweet, blissful moments, I am lost.

Then reason takes over. This isn't right. I shouldn't be kissing anyone now, not until I figure out who I want; Jax or Rey; and it can't be both.

Placing my palms firmly against his chest, I press him away, keeping my gaze down because I am ashamed of myself.

"I can't, Rey," I whisper, shifting backward on the stone step so a giant space full of awkward tension swells between us.

For a long time he says nothing. I can feel his eyes burning into the top of my skull while he pieces everything together. It's not like it's a difficult puzzle to map out.

"Kelsey," he eventually says very slowly, as if I won't understand that it's my name. "What is your relationship with Jax?"

He doesn't sound hurt or angry. He doesn't sound like anything at all, reminding me of the blank voice of the Gamble calling out numbers. It makes me feel worse because it means he's trying to control his emotions to not upset me. I wish he'd yell instead. Someone needs to scream some sense into my brain because I suck at it.

Sighing, I chew my lips that still tingle from Rey's kiss. The moment of truth has arrived. "I don't know."

"You don't know?"

"It's complicated. It's... I don't know."

"Have you kissed him?"

"Yes."

"Do you love him?"

"No. Maybe. I don't know."

"Do you love me?"

I look at Rey again, finding his dazzling blue eyes that are the same color as the sky at noon on a beautiful sunny day. Except now storm clouds hover behind them, dark and ominous.

"Of course I love you, Rey."

"But not the way you love Jax?"

"I don't know!" I cry. "I don't even know if I love Jax!"

"So what do you know?" he demands, his voice rising as he scowls and leans away. And somehow we are fighting again, the second day in a row with someone I had almost never fought with at all before, and certainly never fought with over anything important.

Squirming on the step, my fingers twist and knot together, mimicking my rolling insides. "I know that I care about both of you and that right now, I need some time alone to figure out everything. Figure out what I'm feeling. So much has happened."

"But you love me, Kelsey." It comes out as a desperate plea, his face crumpling, and I'd rather he go back to being angry.

"But I think I might love him too. I never meant for it to happen. I hated him in the beginning and he hated me, but... but you were dead Rey and it damn near killed me. I had to find a way to live again."

Shoving to his feet, he glares down at me, angelic features twisted in pain and anger. "Well, you certainly didn't waste any time."

"Rey-" but he's gone, vanishing through the door and into the building before I can even figure out what I wanted to say next.

CHAPTER SIX

Dropping my head into my hands, I wrap my fingers into my hair and tug, as if that will relieve some of the pressure building inside my head threatening to explode. I feel like absolute crap, like the scum of the earth, and I have no idea where to go. I can't stay in the dorm suite with Jax, not after sleeping beside him last night and not when I'll only feel guilty about Rey. I don't know what old dorm suite Rey was assigned to, but I can't stay with him because then I'll only feel guilty about Jax. The shame gnaws at my gut like a ravenous rodent. It may well eat me alive before I figure out what to do about any of this.

More fireflies flit across the open field before me, glowing and twinkling in the dark as they drift from the tall grass. The moon hasn't traveled high enough yet, the sky still dark. I enjoy the solemn blackness dotted only with the twinkling stars and the shimmering twist of the Milky Way.

A shape trots from the tree line and a few moments later Tisis appears, fur shining silver in the starlight. A dead squirrel hangs from her teeth, which she drops on the steps by my feet as if offering it to me for dinner.

"What? Are we friends now?" I ask her. She cocks her head to one side, eyes glittering and ears pricked forward.

"Go take it to Jax," I say, pointing to the open door of the apartment complex. She snatches up her kill and slinks inside, padded paws silent on the concrete and floor tiles.

"Well hey there, poppet."

I twist around to see the giant, hulking form of Ryder

striding through the door, his thick, wide shoulders brushing the frame. A gun is slung across his back and he's dressed all in black with a lantern swinging in one hand. He must have been assigned night security, which has been doubled since our attack on the League. Even though they probably won't plan retaliation this quickly; not with the condition in which we left them; Nole and Charlie take the 'safe over sorry' method of protection. I have no arguments.

"Hi," I say, staring straight up from where I sit as he stops beside me, his large boots coming up to my shoulders. The lantern casts glowing patterns across the stairs around me.

"You on security tonight?" he asks, his bald head shining in the small bit of candlelight escaping from the inside entry hall.

I go to say no, but realize I have nothing else to do. Having slept all day, I'm not tired and I've already established I have nowhere to go. Jumping to my feet, I flick my hair out of my face. "Yes."

Looking me up and down, Ryder inspects my attire. "Shorts and a tank top? Don't look like you're ready."

I glance at my bare feet and pajamas. "Give me five minutes."

"You got three. I'm not sittin' round waitin' for you to make yourself pretty."

Nodding that I understand, I charge up the stairs to suite 307. Flinging open the door, I find Nadia and Jax sitting at the tiny kitchenette counter eating dinner. A full plate, still warm, waits for me and yet another twinge of remorse stabs into my heart as they both stare at me expectantly.

"I'm on security detail," I say quickly, rushing to the bathroom to find new clothes and my boots. Changing in a few seconds into cargo pants and a clean shirt, I pull my unruly curls into a ponytail with a thin strip of leather and yank the bath-room door back open.

Jax stands in the doorway and I startle, jumping back-ward with one hand flying to my chest.

"No, you aren't," he says flatly, ignoring my reaction.

"What?"

"You aren't on security detail tonight. I assign security now and didn't pick you because you need to rest and I don't feel you're ready to face the League again."

"I'm going anyway. With Ryder."

Pressing past him, disregarding his narrowed eyes, I grab a handgun from his stash in the living room, tuck it into the waistband of my pants and then return to the kitchen to ruffle Nadia's hair, give her a quick hug and tweak her tiny nose that looks like someone stuck a leftover piece of putty on her face. "We'll have dinner together tomorrow, ok? Just you and me."

She pouts for a moment and then shrugs. "Be careful."

I almost find it funny that a child is worried about my well-being when it should be the other way around.

"Of course I will. Besides, after what we did to the League, they have bigger problems than me right now."

Tisis sits at her feet, yellow-green eyes watching every movement. After thinking for a moment, I pat the wolf on the head, her fur coarse and thick. She lets me do so without even so much as a growl. I think Tisis and I have finally come to a friendly arrangement, much better than the first night we met when I thought she was going to rip my throat out. At least someone around here doesn't hate me.

I duck of the the door and into the empty hallway when a strong hand around my elbow drives me to a halt.

"What's going on?" Jax demands as I spin to face him.

Closing the apartment door to spare Nadia whatever heavy discussion comes next, he folds his arms over his broad chest and regards me with cool challenge across his features.

"What do you mean?" My voice comes out as a small squeak instead of the nonchalant question I had envisioned. I clear my throat and shuffle my feet uncomfortably, reaching for my mother's necklace that I have somehow managed to not lose in everything that's happened.

Jax's jaw grinds together. "I mean, you are not only volunteering for night security, you're actually happy it about it. I'm the only person who's ever happy about night security. And Ryder."

"Good for you?"

"What happened with Rey?"

"Nothing," I lie and hope he doesn't see through it. Trying to leave again, he stops me a second time by sliding between me and the stairway door.

"What do you want?" I snap in anger, which is misplaced, I know. I'm mad at myself and taking it out on Jax, using security detail as an excuse to not have to talk to him tonight and explain why we can't share a bed, why he can't kiss me anymore. More time for me to think. More time to delay the inevitable decision.

"I saw you." His tone is soft, but the words come out as the accusation they are. "I saw you kiss Rey."

And suddenly my heart has dropped into my stomach and my tongue has turned as dry as sandpaper and tripled in size. Anything I had planned to say flees my mind, leaving it blank.

"You're spying on me?" I manage to spit out, the question harsher than I intended and certainly not the best response. None of my words are coming out right and it only adds to the anxiety swirling inside me.

"No. I went down to let you know dinner was ready and to invite your *best friend* to join us."

"Jax, it's not what you think."

"So then what is it?"

"Complicated," I say, cringing because that's apparently the only word I know anymore.

"Were you planning on telling me?"

"Yes. Eventually. I just needed time to think."

"If I tried to kiss you right now, would you let me?"

"No."

A long, weighty silence falls over us and I swear it will suffocate me, choking off my oxygen with its oppression. Animosity rolls off of Jax in waves and for a brief second I wonder if he'll snap, if this will be the final straw Daniel had been so concerned about.

Jax watches me, I can feel his gaze driving into my skull as if he's trying to read my mind. Good luck, I'd love to know what I'm thinking. I'm yet again staring at the floor of cracked and missing tiles, unable to look him in the eye because I'll only start crying and make everything worse. I can't cry, not when I'm the one causing everyone to be hurt and angry. I have no right to be sad.

"I guess it's not so complicated then," he finally growls before re-entering the apartment and slamming the door in my face. On its single screw, the upside-down "7" wavers back and forth with little swish sounds.

* * *

"That was longer than three minutes," Ryder says as I re-emerge into the night.

"Sorry."

His face scrunches. "You cryin'?"

I hastily wipe at my cheeks, having not even noticed they were wet. "No." More lies. I guess that's all I'm capable of tonight.

"I don't deal with women cryin'."

"I'm not."

"Good. Find a way to toughen up, poppet, you're gonna need it in this world. Apple?"

Offering me the shiny green fruit, I take it from his giant, scarred hand as my mouth waters. I'm starving and I really need to remember to eat more consistently. With everything going on, with the war that marches closer to our doorstep, I need to keep my strength and I've definitely gotten too thin after being half-starved by the League. My ribs stick out and my collar bone protrudes and if Elsa saw me now, she'd sit me in a chair and feed me until I burst.

Crisp and delicious, the apple's juice dribbles down my chin as I bite into it. Food on the surface tastes so much better than the food in ROC ever did, even without the spices and sauces and elaborate means to prepare it that I'd been accustomed to in the O.Z. Maybe because most of the food in ROC is genetically engineered, or not nearly as fresh or it's all pumped so full of preservatives and chemicals I'm not even sure it can be considered food anymore, but either way, I enjoy the change.

Staying close to the massive man, I trail him from the property and into the woods. I'm amazed that he moves so quiet and graceful, barely unsettling the ground or shrubbery without having to slow his pace. Everyone up here walks like that, except me of course, crashing through the underbrush like a moron.

Finishing the apple, I toss the core into the shrubs.

"Shouldn'ta done that," he says.

"Why not?"

"Someone finds it, they'll know we're close and possibly which way we went."

"Oh, I never even thought of that. I'm sorry."

"Don't be sorry, just learn. You got a gun?" he asks, swinging his lantern around. I lift the hem of my shirt to display the weapon. He thins his lips and glares. "Why the heck isn't it in your hand then? We're on security, kiddo. And I'm willing to bet some of the League'll be lookin' for us already. Especially you. In case you haven't noticed, you're on their hit list. Sawyer's probably got a fancy price on your head."

Scrambling, I jerk the gun from my pants and wrap my hands around it the way Jax had taught, safety off and right index finger hovering over the trigger.

Ryder jumps to the side. "Oh, come on, poppet! Don't walk around with your finger on the trigger. That's a good way to shoot someone you don't mean to. Keep it along the side of the barrel n'only move to the trigger when you're certain of what you're 'bout to kill. This thing's no toy."

Making the adjustment, I look to Ryder for approval. Giving me a once over, he nods. "You know how to use it?"

"I've killed four people." There's no emotion in my voice as I say it, as if I have detached myself from my crimes, justified or otherwise. Still, however calm I might appear on the outside, their deaths weigh heavy on my conscious and chew on my bones. Their ghosts didn't leave this earth and now cling to my back, sit on my shoulders and haunt my mind. I wonder if they will ever go away.

Ryder stares at me long and hard, the lantern raised between us so the light falls on his tan, sun-worn face. "You did what you had to, to be standin' here today. There's no shame in that and don't think for a second any of those people would feel guilty if they had killed you instead."

"I know. I just don't want to become a monster," I say, thinking of Jax's words.

"Then don't become a monster. In this world, you choose who you become."

"Can you teach Nadia to use a gun?" The words burst from my mouth before I've even realized I'm thinking about them. Ryder blinks with surprise.

"The little girl you brought back? She's a child."

"I can't imagine someone's age would stop you. She needs to learn. I can't always be there to protect her. Or Jax. She's really smart and mature and the League probably wants her nearly as bad as they want me."

"And why can't you or Jaxon teach her?"

"Because I'm surprised I haven't shot myself in the foot yet and Jax... he... well, I'd prefer if it were you." I don't feel like going into the personal details of my life with Ryder, especially not right now.

"I'm not teachin' a little girl how to fire a weapon. We try real hard to not turn the kids around here into soldiers. This life is already hard enough. Maybe in a few more years."

"Do you have children of your own, Ryder?"

He stands taller, shoulders square. A muscle in his jaw twitches. "As a matter of fact I do. Two sons, one's Ivan who I think you've met. Aside from the fact that you don't got children and aren't even old enough to be Nadia's mother anyway."

"She has no one else and we're both from ROC. I'm the best she's got and I want to make sure she'll be safe when the League comes."

"She'll be safe," he assures. Somehow, he says it with such

conviction, I actually believe him. I duck my head with shame because I know he's right. Nadia has no business handling a gun. The world has already stolen enough of her innocence. I don't need to extinguish the rest.

"I just worry about her," I say.

"She's lucky to have you. From what I've seen she's a strong and smart kid, and Jaxon's wolf seems to have taken' a likin' to her. She'll be ok. You're gonna have bigger things to worry 'bout."

Sighing, I rake a hand through my ponytail and nod in agreement. He has no idea.

"Can we patrol the perimeter now?" he asks. "This conversation's gettin' too heart-to-heart for me as it is."

Without another word, I trudge along behind him through the dark forest with only a single lantern to guide us. We walk in silence, Ryder because he appears to be a man of few words and me because I'm lost in my thoughts of Jax and Rey and how they're now both angry with me and I don't know how to make this situation better. If I choose to be with Rey, Jax will be hurt and if I choose to be with Jax, Ray will be crushed and either way, I'll feel nothing but guilt. I suppose I could choose neither of them, but I don't know if that will help anything.

I think about how it wouldn't be a problem if Rey were actually dead. I had come to terms with that and had learned to somehow move on. Then I feel sick to my stomach for even considering such an awful idea. What kind of horrible person am I? I couldn't be happier he's back, it's all I could have hoped for a month ago and I would never change it now. I just wish I'd known the truth before I met Jax. I wish I could have known a lot of things. I wish people hadn't kept so many secrets from me.

"Oof!" I'm so consumed by the trouble swirling through my mind, I don't realize Ryder has stopped walking and blown out the lantern until I plow into him.

"Shh!" he commands and I can only assume he glares at me even though I can't see anything in the darkness as my eyes adjust to the loss of lantern light. "There's people up ahead, 'bout two hundred yards."

I'd love to know how he can possibly assess whether or not there are people so far ahead in the quiet blackness of the woods, but I also know he's far more adept at this than I'll ever be.

"They're comin' this way," he whispers, leaning down so he can speak against my ear.

"Is it the League? Do we hide? How many are there?" Questions pour from my lips, one after another until he places a giant hand over my mouth to silence me.

"Probably. No. And it sounds like two. I imagine the League has teams wanderin' the woods tryin' to figure out where we all ran off to. Or they know we're with the Risers now and are comin' to see what they're up against."

Now I can hear them, soft footsteps crunching on the dense underbrush, the faint snap of a tree branch or rustle of leaves. If I hadn't known to stop and listen, I'd have strolled right into them.

With terror plastered over my face, blood frozen in my veins, I cast a hurried glance at Ryder.

"This would be a good time to put your finger on the trigger," he directs, his gruff voice so quiet I almost can't hear him at all. I switch to the trigger, my hand quaking at the thought I might be killing another person tonight.

CHAPTER SEVEN

The tension hovering over us fills the air, oppressive and dense. I shift nervously until Ryder shoots me a look that freezes me in place.

"Don't do anythin' till I say otherwise," he instructs, though I almost can't hear him over the chaotic thrashing of my heart.

Personally, I'd rather just turn and run away, but they'll definitely hear me crashing through the woods like a lunatic. And what if they follow us back to the Risers' compound? I'll never risk my friends like that.

With a grip on my arm, Ryder twists us into the shadows of the trees as two figures materialize along the thin path, almost invisible in their black clothing.

"I swear I heard voices," one says, the deep voice and wide shoulders identifying him as a man. Judging by the petit size of the other person, it's unquestionably a woman. I can tell by their military-like clothing that they're League, but they seem more uncertain and less confident than the other League scouts I've dealt with, like they're unaccustomed to patrolling the woods in the dark. Maybe they're newbies since we killed so many of the better-trained patrols. At least we have one thing going for us. Plus, I'm with Ryder. He's the equivalent of three well-trained League members.

But even with him beside me, a thick, muscular arm locked around my body and pinning me to the tree so I'm guarded from any stray gunfire, I can still feel the fear and alarm unfurl up through my chest. If I had a choice, I'd rather deal with the Gendarme officers every day for the remainder of my life than ever confront a League member again.

Of course, as luck would have it...

As the two people pass, unaware of our presence, Ryder slides from behind the tree, fluid and lithe. I follow, praying I don't make any noise by stepping on a twig or smacking a shin into a rock or some other stupid mistake. My silence doesn't matter though because a half second later I hear the now unpleasantly familiar click of a gun cocking.

Ryder, finger on the trigger, has leveled his weapon at the back of the man's head. "I suggest you don't move."

Both League members halt and stiffen, their tension visible even in the poor moonlight that manages to infiltrate the trees. With a hefty sigh, I lift and cock my gun too, aiming for the woman.

Please don't let me have to kill anyone tonight. I can't handle any more death, even if it is the League. I'm tired of washing blood from my hands only to have it return in my nightmares.

The man reaches for his own gun and Ryder nudges the barrel of his weapon into the base of the man's skull. "Nope. Now drop your weapons," Ryder commands, his voice booming and authoritative and sounding almost exactly like my father.

Neither move. Ryder jams his gun harder into the man's neck, causing him to flinch. "I said drop them!"

Guns clatter to the ground as the man and woman raise their now empty hands over their heads.

"There's more of us out here," the man sneers.

"Fantastic. If we happen to come across any that seem more interestin', I'll just shoot you and take them," Ryder replies coolly. I have no doubt he will. I wonder, though, where he intends to take these two people. Back to the Risers' boarding-school-turned-compound? Is that safe, or even wise? Where will we put them and what use does he think two League members will be anyway? But we can't just kill them and we definitely can't let them go. A million questions collide through my brain, but I don't want to ask Ryder and make the League minions think we're unplanned and unprepared. Or that I'm an idiot.

"Now, we're gonna start walkin' and if either of you try anything funny, Kelsey here is gonna shoot you in the leg. I'm sure you know who she is by now and that she's already killed four of your people in the brief time she's been on the surface. At that rate, her track record will be better than mine within a year."

Both captives regard me with interest and I try to look menacing, scowling the way Jax did when he once stood before Elijah in my defense. I hope I look intimidating.

Without warning, the man's right arm lashes out, catching the tip of Ryder's gun. The weapon fires, but with Ryder taken off guard, it now aims at the sky. From a nearby tree, birds shriek and scatter as the bullet tears through several leaves, sending a flurry of leafy remains fluttering to the ground.

Striking again, the man catches Ryder in the throat directly above his Adam's apple. Ryder staggers backward, choking and gasping for air as his eyes bulge and one hand flies to his neck.

The woman dives at me, arms outstretched and before I can react or just have a moment to think, I've fired my gun. She recoils and topples into a thick tree trunk with a howl of pain. Even in the darkness, I see the shimmer of blood as it pumps from her shoulder and spills down her armor; a black, wet, dancing ribbon.

I whip around to face the men, leveling my gun in time to see Ryder land a fist square to the League man's jaw. The man drops to his knees, shaking his head in disorientation and spitting blood to the ground. Ryder adjusts his gun, holding it directly against the man's forehead and I suck in my breath, wanting to look away, but unable to do so, dread filling me with cement and holding me steadfast and solid.

I'm suddenly reminded of Ashlynn, the way the bullet exploded through her head that night Daniel was killed. I wince at the gruesome image ingrained in my mind. One I will never forget

"What the hell did I just say?" Ryder demands, his voice raspy from the man's blow, but somehow still calm, though now a harsh coldness laces his words.

"Do it," the man says, glaring up at Ryder in defiance, the same defiance I once showed Elijah knowing he'd probably kill me no matter what I said or did. It's the strength of someone ready to die when no other options are left. The understanding that sometimes death is better than whatever else the future might hold.

Ryder's gun clicks as he re-cocks the trigger and my body turns cold as I watch in horror. Surely Ryder wouldn't, not an unarmed prisoner. But his face remains impassive and terror grips at my heart. The world around me tunnels, the League man's face all I can see as I realize I will watch him die.

Then Ryder changes his aim and fires, hitting the man in the same shoulder in which I shot the woman. The man grunts and falls against the earth, one hand clutching the wound as he writhes and kicks at the ground with his legs. A string of curse words launches from his lips.

"Good call on shooting their shoulders, Kelsey," Ryder says. "If we shoot 'em in the leg then they can't walk. I wasn't even thinkin'. Now, both of you get up and if you try anythin' stupid like that again, the next bullet really does go in your head."

I can only stare in horrified shock. Not at the injured man, but at Ryder, who pulled the trigger and wounded someone who knelt unarmed and defenseless before him. I know it's the League and I know they attacked us first, but this fight was over, we were safe. Shooting our prisoner, that was just out of spite. It's something the bad guy does, something I watched Sawyer and Elijah do, but not something my friends are supposed to do. Not when we're supposed to be the good guys. Without realizing, I inch backward, away from Ryder.

The League woman sobs, but the League man grits his teeth against the burning pain, rising to his feet and yanking the woman to hers.

"Grab their guns, kiddo," Ryder says. I don't move, too horrified to do anything other than stare.

"Kid!" Ryder growls. "I said grab their guns."

I shove my thoughts of disgust aside and scramble for the two extra weapons, swinging both over my shoulder and around my back before retraining my own gun on our prisoners. The added weight forces me to lean at an uncomfortable angle, but Ryder has already begun to head towards the new compound, our prisoners staggering ahead of him.

I follow at a distance, not wanting to be too close to a man who shoots people for no reason. Within minutes, my arm grows sore and tired from holding my weapon steady, but I refuse to allow the gun to waiver so much as an inch. I hope Ryder doesn't notice my apprehension of our captives. Even with him here, and the knowledge that he will only allow the League to take me over his dead body, it doesn't appease my nerves. They've killed over much less, and my views on Ryder have suddenly shifted.

Ryder guides us through the woods in silence. If our male prisoner told the truth and there are other League members in the woods tonight, we don't encounter them. Eventually the large brick building I left earlier comes into view, a tiny beacon of golden candlelight on the first floor.

As usual, guards are stationed out front and patrolling the edge of the forest. As we approach and they see we have prisoners, one immediately rushes inside calling for Nole and Charlie. The other, an older man with a complexion as dark as Daniel's, frowns. "And what exactly are we supposed to do with them?"

"Whatever Nole and Charlie deem best," Ryder replies, prodding the League members with his gun and forcing them to kneel. Both glower, but drop to the ground upon seeing little room to argue. Sweat beads along their pale, grey-tinged skin. They've lost a lot of blood and I'm sure they're in a lot of pain. Without medical attention, it's possible Nole and Charlie won't have to decide what to do.

"I don't like it," the other man replies, lips drawn into a tight line and eyebrows knit together, but he says nothing else and moments later Nole and Charlie appear on the front steps, backlit from the lanterns hanging inside.

"Found 'em about a mile away in the woods," Ryder says. "I shot one, Kelsey shot the other. They'll need to see Camrie if we plan to keep 'em alive."

Nole looks at both our prisoners, then at me, the hint of amusement glittering in his jet-black eyes. "Well, this is an interesting role reversal."

"This whole surface adventure is just one interesting episode after another," I reply with an exasperated sigh, lowering my gun and offering the two weapons we took off the League members to a nearby guard.

"I guess we should lock them up somewhere," Charlie says, lifting an eyebrow in Nole's direction as if seeking approval.

He shrugs. "Up to you. The League has been terrorizing

your people far more than mine these last few weeks and it's your team that caught them."

Charlie steps closer to the prisoners, brushing long, auburn hair from her face. "If we keep them here, Sawyer will send more to get them back."

"Sawyer's sending men to find us anyway," Ryder announces. "I figure it's why these clowns were in the woods in the first place."

The small crowd that has started to form shifts with unease and a few sideways glances. With a slight nod, Charlie chews her thin bottom lip. "And if we kill them, Sawyer will add it to his list of reasons for revenge against us, which seems to have already grown quite long."

"So? Like I said, they're comin' either way," Ryder says again.

Everyone is silent for several tense moments as we watch Charlie. I can't understand how she must feel, weighing the safety of her people against killing two others in cold blood. With them both injured and weaponless, it would no longer be in self-defense but would become an execution, something I can't foresee Charlie ever being able to justify. I hope she doesn't, I hope she lets them live. I know I shouldn't, but I can't have a second person tonight make me question the side on which I stand. We aren't the League and we aren't ROC. We can't execute people for being in the wrong place at the wrong time.

Several curious Risers and some of our own compound members have stepped from the apartment. Behind this growing group of people I don't know, I see the shiny black hair of Randolph and Evy... standing beside Jax.

A twinge of sadness passes through me at the knowledge he didn't come running to my side, that I wouldn't have known he were there at all if I hadn't scanned the small throng forming. His eyes catch mine and I hastily look away. What do I expect from him anyway after what I've done? Of course he doesn't want to be with me.

Everyone talks in hushed whispers, eyes darting between Charlie, Nole and our captives. I catch pieces of individual debates. Most don't want the League members to live, and no one looks happy at all that Ryder brought them here.

Then a figure brushes through the crowd and my stomach flip-flops when I recognize Rey's golden hair.

Stepping forward and circling around Ryder, he moves to stand beside me, his fingers lacing into mine. Without hesitation, I shake him off, jamming my hands into my pockets, his presence beside me causing more anxiety than comfort. The hurt on his face tear at my insides. I refuse to meet his gaze, instead casting a nervous glance at Jax, whose face has darkened into a deep scowl. So now everyone's mad at me. At least I'm consistent.

I assume Jax will storm away, but Charlie begins to speak again and everyone turns their attention to her.

"I'm not executing two people, whatever some of you may think, so we might as well lock them up."

"Seriously?" a man demands, fury written on his features. "After everything the League has done to us?"

"Yes, seriously. If you have a problem with it, Nathan, I'm happy to discuss it privately."

The man spits on the ground at the League's feet. "Weak. That's what you're becoming, ever since that damn Sub showed up."

"Hey!" Nole shouts, but the man, Nathan, has already stormed away, several others following him in solidarity, all casting furious looks at Charlie over their shoulders.

"Let him go," Charlie says with a flick of her hand. "There's no point arguing with anyone over this, he's entitled to his opinion. Meanwhile, we can use the guys as hostages when Elijah and his men figure out where Kelsey and the rest of my compound are hiding. I have no illusions that it won't be soon."

CHAPTER EIGHT

People glance at each other as Charlie voices what we don't want to admit. Some eye the woods with trepidation. With the League already patrolling the area, we can't argue another battle stalks closer to our doorstep. After our last attack, we'd be lying to ourselves if we say we didn't see this coming. Not that it makes the idea sit any better in my head.

Jax shifts from the crowd, ignoring my presence as if I have somehow gone invisible in the last few minutes. It's so infuriating I'm tempted to jump in front of him and knock him on the nose or yell and scream until he acknowledges that I'm standing right here.

"Randolph and I will take them to the basement," he offers. "We can take first watch."

"Gee, thanks," Randolph grumbles with a look of discontent, but pulls his gun forward and prods at the League man. "Let's go, buddy."

"Hold on!" someone barks and it takes me a second to realize it's Rey. He moves forward to stand between Jax and Charlie, brow furrowed. "These people nearly killed Kelsey. Twice. And you want to just lock them up? What if they escape? And what do we do when the League arrives anyway? It's time to come up with a plan rather than protect the enemy. I'm not going to sit around and watch Kelsey placed in danger a third time with the League. I say we shoot them."

I'm rendered speechless at Rey's actions and his words, so out of character from the goofy, kind Rey I grew up with. The

Rey that willingly added his number to the Gamble hundreds of times so others could survive, regardless of the outcome to himself. He'd never advocate to kill anyone, but this new Rey, I don't know what to think of him as he stands tall before Charlie.

"That's not really your choice to make," Nole says, voice stern and even.

Rey flips around, showing no intimidation from Nole. "Why not? It'll affect me won't it? I'm one of you now. So is Kelsey. Shouldn't we all vote on what happens to these two?"

Charlie's brow furrows. "There's plenty I allow my people to vote on, but this won't be one of those things. Not with emotions as high as they are right now around here. At the end of the day, my compound is not a democracy."

"So it's a dictatorship?" Rey demands. "Awesome. The surface isn't any better than ROC. A handful of people deciding they know what's best for everyone while putting all out lives in danger."

"Well, if you want to shoot them in cold blood right now, here you go," Jax replies with cool nonchalance, offering his gun to Rey. Rey looks between the weapon and the two prisoners, mouth half open.

My throat clenches because he's actually considering this as an option. And I don't know whether or not I should try to stop him. It'll be two less League people to worry about. Then I hate myself for even thinking about killing them the same way Sawyer killed those ROC citizens. No one deserves a blatant execution except for maybe Sawyer and Elijah themselves. Killing these two won't stop the League's mission and it won't stop them from seeking their revenge. If anything, it will add to their mounting list of grievances.

Rey still hasn't moved. Nor has anyone else. And I'm holding my breath because a month ago I would have never believed Rey capable of something like this and now I'm not sure what to think.

"Yeah, didn't think so," Jax says after a long tense silence when Rey doesn't take the gun. Jax slides it back into his holster. I exhale with relief.

"Fine, but what's being done to keep Kelsey safe?" Rey demands, eyes flashing as he steps closer to Jax.

"Kelsey has taken care of herself on more than one occasion," Jax says and I'm taken aback that he defends me... kind of... all things considered.

"Like the two times the League had her locked up?" Rey demands. "Like when they drugged her and beat her and would have killed her?"

"Well, fortunately those two times, I was here to save her," Jax says, his expression smug. "Unlike you. Now get out of my face before you regret it, Sub."

"Why don't you get out of mine?" With two hands, Rey pushes Jax's broad shoulders, causing him to stumble backward.

"Rey!" I exclaim with a step forward. Neither listen as Jax shoves him back, both their faces distorted in ugly rage.

It happens so quickly, I have no idea who threw the first punch. Before I can even stop them, Jax and Rey wrestle on the ground, fists slinging every direction as strings of profanity spit from both their mouths. Blood gushes from Rey's nose and Jax's lip, though neither seems to be gaining an upper hand on the other as they roll across the grass, flailing and thrashing, jabbing fists and knees whenever an opportunity presents itself.

"Stop it!" I scream, rushing toward them as Randolph and Nole do the same. Everyone else stares in startled surprise, mouths agape, unsure how to react. Randolph grabs the back of Jax's T-shirt, tearing the collar as he struggles to get a grip on Jax. Meanwhile, Nole fights Rey away, hauling him to his feet and giving him a rough shake from both shoulders.

Blood paints Rey's face like a gruesome piece of artwork, his nose clearly broken, one cheek cut and a black eye already forming. As Randolph yanks Jax to his feet, I see he doesn't look any better with at least one bottom tooth chipped and blood flowing from his mouth. He spits a clump to the ground and wipes at his chin.

And then both boys are shouting. Nole and Charlie are shouting. Everyone is shouting, the sound deafening to my ears.

"Are you completely insane?" I cry, storming up to Rey and pushing him with both hands.

"He started it!" Rey barks, running the back of his hand across his nose and jabbing a blood coated finger at Jax.

"I didn't start crap you idiot, Sub!" Jax replies another glob of blood spattering from his mouth while he fights against Randolph, and now Ryder, who struggle to restrain him.

"Enough!" roars Nole, his voice booming over everyone else and stunning the crowd into silence. "Rey! You're coming with me! Jaxon go with Ryder. And if either of you so much as look at each other the wrong way I'll toss you in the cell with the League members!"

I've forgotten about them. Flipping around, I see both still kneeling, their hands bound. The woman stares wide-eyed and trembles. The man sneers at me. "You just have all kinds of people fighting over you, don't you, Sub?" Then he throws back his head and laughs, the kind that vibrates his whole chest.

Without thinking, I stride forward, lift a leg, and kick him square in the stomach. He coughs and gags, crumpling forward.

Suddenly there's a firm grip on my arm. Turning, Charlie stands beside me, her face tight and angry as her eyes bore into mine. "Stop. And come with me."

Her tone leaves no room for argument, nor do her fingers wrapped around my elbow as she all but hauls me into the building, down the main hall and into one of the empty class-rooms lining the back of the building.

Once inside, Charlie sets about lighting extra lanterns and candles throughout the space, desks and chairs so coated in dust I doubt anyone has touched them in years. The soft, gold light does nothing to make Charlie appear less ominous and I shrink into a corner of the room hoping she'll forget she dragged me here.

She doesn't.

"What was all that about?" she demands, voice sharp and challenging as she whips to face me.

"What does he think he knows about anything? I wanted that stupid smile off his face!" I'm shaking and hot, skin flushed as my blood boils.

"I'm not talking about the League prisoner, though I thought you were better than that. I'm talking about Jaxon and Rey."

My jaw hinges several times. "I don't know," I reply, shoul-ders curving inward as I slump against the wall, adrenaline flow-ing from my veins and leaving me drained.

Her eyes narrow, full lips thinning into a tight line. "Kel-sey, it was quite clear to everyone out there that Rey and Jax were fighting about more than just your safety from the League, so I'm going to ask you one more time, what was that fight actu-ally about?"

"I... they..." I stammer, fumbling for words when there aren't any good ones I can use to explain. Anything I say makes me sound like a horrible person. Maybe I am.

Charlie leans on a long desk at the front of the room, her palms resting on the scratched, chipped surface. Behind her, a white board with notes of some sort of chemical reaction drawn across it hangs dented and dirty on the wall. It occurs to me that lesson has been there for a century, someone's painstaking work for a final class before they likely never taught again.

She pieces together her next words carefully. "In ROC, what was your relationship with Rey?"

"We were best friends. We grew up together."

Her head cocks to one side. "And then it became something more?"

I lick my lips. "Yes. I guess. It was after his number was selected in the Gamble. I mean, he always loved me more than a friend, he wanted to marry me. I just didn't realize I felt the same way until he was sentenced to death."

"So you love him?"

"Yes."

"And what about Jax?" I expect her question to be harsher; she has a stronger connection to Jax than Rey; but it's not. She asks with a calm indifference that has become so familiar to the way she handles most situations, as if she has to detach herself from any emotion to arrive at a logical conclusion. As if detachment is the only way to survive anything in her world.

I sigh, turning my gaze to the dingy plaster wall behind a sink in the far corner, cracked and missing tiles cover part of the wall behind it. They must have once been white along with the paint on the wall. Now everything only boosts shades of brown and grey, all framed in mold and mildew.

"I love him too."

It's the first time I've ever admitted my feelings out loud. Now that I have, I know how true they are. It doesn't seem possible, and I don't even know how it happened, but I am in love with two men; equally and irrevocably.

Charlie nods slowly, chewing on her bottom lip. "It's the eyes isn't it?"

I return my gaze to Charlie. "What?"

"Their eyes. Both boys have gorgeous blue eyes. I can see why you fell for them. I was a sucker for eyes once. Green though. Like the color of the grass in early spring, right when the snow melts and everything is fresh and alive. They made me feel alive too. Every time I looked at him, I found myself hoping our children would have his beautiful eyes."

She seems lost in thought, her own eyes drifting to stare out the dark windows and into the night beyond, though I don't think it's the darkness she sees.

"What happened to him?" I ask.

Shaking her head, a sorrow washes over her face that I've never seen before, not even on my father's when my mother was selected and he escorted her to the chambers. It drags my heart, as if her grief holds a tangible force that has the ability to tear a person to shreds.

"He gone. It doesn't matter anymore. But Jax and Rey are here, dealing with this mess right now. That you caused."

"I know."

"Then you know you have to choose. You can't do this to both of them. Not because it's not fair, though it isn't, but because it will rip them apart. If they don't rip each other apart first."

"I know," I say again, hanging my head because I am humiliated. "It's just so hard. Rey, he was dead. If I had even the slightest indication that he were still alive, if I had known anything at all, I would have never developed feelings for Jax."

"You were able to control your feelings?"

"Well, no, but... I don't know. It would have been different. I could have made different choices."

"Kelsey, life rarely hands us easy choices, and almost never the choices we want. Most of them will be a challenge, and some will be so difficult and conflicting, they'll shred you to pieces from the inside out before you figure out what you want, or what is best for those you care about."

"So what do I do?"

"I can't tell you that. You have to figure it out for yourself, and preferably before they kill each other."

We stand in silence for almost a full minute before Charlie turns to the door.

"I'm going to check with Nole and Ryder, make sure everyone is calmed down. The Risers have a last spare suite upstairs in the dorms, 319. You can stay there as long as you need. I think the solitude will help you think a little better." She floats through the door, shutting it behind her until the latch clicks.

It's a long time before I move again, and only to find the room she spoke of to collapse into a bed.

Sleep doesn't come as easily as it should, especially considering all I have been through the past week. Instead, I lay in the dark and stare at the stained ceiling, arms folded behind my head, deep in thought over Rey and Jax and who I should choose, or if I should choose neither.

With Jax, everything is new and exciting. It's hopeful and holds no reminders of my life below the surface, only of the freedom I have found. He's saved me. I've saved him. Somehow, deep inside our cores, we are the same person living in fear of being alone, of losing the ones we love more than we fear losing ourselves. Our personal demons make us one. We complete each other, like two halves of an apple.

But with Rey it is familiar and comfortable, like a favorite sweater. We've always been together and a part of me thought we always would be. I have a history with him, memories of happiness like when we were six and made a fort out of pillows and blankets and living room furniture and pretended it was our home. Or when we were ten and played games imagining we lived on the surface before the war.

Or when I first said I loved him.

I did love him. I do. But I love Jax too. I don't understand how it's possible to love two people so much and I can feel it filling my heart until it strains at the seams, threatening to burst if I do nothing about it. A ticking time bomb lurking inside my chest.

I have to choose, I know I do, but I don't know how. Whichever one I pick, the other will be hurt which means I will hurt too. I can't repair my heart by breaking someone else's. I love them both. I need them both. I can't live in a world where they aren't both here beside me. It's selfish and I hate myself for doing this to them because it isn't fair. Jax and Rey, they deserve so much better.

CHAPTER NINE

My stomach twists around itself and I'm so anxious I might be sick as I stand in front of the door. I debate just leaving, no one has seen me yet, but a promise is a promise so I reach up and knock twice.

As I anticipated, Jax opens the door. If my appearance at all surprises him, he doesn't show it, greeting me with a stone-cold expression reminiscent of the first time I ever saw him when he just wanted to shoot me. I wonder if he ever wishes he had.

His face has transformed into a purple mess of new bruises and swollen cuts from his fight with Rey. I can't image Rey looks any better and I feel the persistent gnaw of guilt chew harder.

"I wanted to see if Nadia wants to have dinner with me since we didn't eat together last night," I say, my words rushing out all at once so it sounds less like English and more like random, garbled noise.

Jax doesn't move, or even open his mouth and I'm about to repeat myself when Nadia comes bolting from the bedrooms, around the kitchen counter and straight for me. Tisis follows behind on silent paws, tongue lolling from her mouth and staying no more than a few paces behind the little girl.

"Hey, Nadia," I say with a warm smile, crouching down so we're eye level and taking both her hands in my own. "You up for that dinner date I promised you last night?"

"Yes!" she says enthusiastically. "And I can show you

something new that Rey taught me!" She scoots around Jax, who has still not said a word, though he continues to stare at me like I'm some sort of intruder. I think about snapping at him with a cruel comment, but I don't want to start an argument in front of Nadia. I'm not going to pretend he doesn't have a right to be mad, but he doesn't have to act like a total jerk about it.

Nadia scoops up a stack of crinkled, yellowed paper from the counter and a partially melted blue wax crayon and then scurries back to me.

"Can Tisis come to?"

Raising an eyebrow, I glance at Jax. He shrugs and turns away to return to the bedrooms. Nadia motions for the wolf, which trots into the hall after us as I swing the door shut, leaving Jax to sit alone in whatever foul mood he's currently dealing with. If this is how he's going to continue to behave, it will make my choice much easier.

"What's for dinner?" Nadia asks as we make our way downstairs to my new apartment.

"Some pork and a vegetable soup. Someone helped me downstairs in the kitchens, though I didn't do much cooking in ROC, so I can't guarantee it will be the best meal you've ever had."

"We didn't really have meals in the O.Z," Nadia replies. "We hardly had enough food for everyone to eat once a day."

My gut wrenches. "What sector were you?"

"D."

"Oh," is all I can say. I'm sure she understands who I am and I can't help but feel guilt at the knowledge I lived in luxury while she barely had enough to survive.

"Are you and Jax fighting?" Nadia asks as we enter my new room and she slides onto a wobbly stool at the tiny counter between the sink and ancient hot plate that doesn't work anymore. Tisis lays on the floor at her feet as I uncover the food brought up from the communal kitchen on the first floor.

I dish out some hot soup and a serving of salted pork. Setting the meal in front of her, I fill a cup of water I pulled from the well this morning. "We aren't fighting."

"Rey says you are. At least that's what he told me when I asked."

My lips mash together as I debate how to explain the situation to a child. "Jax and I aren't fighting, we just... want some time away from each other right now."

"Want to see what Rey taught me?"

"Sure," I say, grateful for a change of subject.

Placing the old paper on the counter, Nadia arranges them in order and I quickly realize it's the alphabet through the letter "M". Picking up the misshapen crayon, she writes in the following letters, "N-O-P" with an unsteady hand, before grinning upward at me with her crooked teeth and a strand of knotted hair partially covering her face.

"I'm learning how to write!"

"Wow, Nadia, that's amazing!" I exclaim, brushing the hair from her eyes. Glancing over the letters, I'm impressed. While I can read and type, I have no idea how to write. Due to space restrictions and the risk of fire, plus the rations, paper hadn't existed in ROC decades, well before I was born. With all systems being electronic anyway, plus our barcodes holding any necessary personal information, there was never a need for anyone to learn to hold a pencil let alone how to write. "And you said Rey taught you this?"

She nods, head down, tongue protruding slightly as she concentrates on forming the next letter. Half paying attention, I take a few bites of my food. It's warm and the pork is slightly overcooked, but overall I managed ok with some help.

I wonder where he learned, how he even found supplies. His mother never taught us, probably didn't even know how herself. Yet one more thing about my best friend that I never knew. How many secrets has he kept from me? Have I ever really known him at all?

A loud pounding on the metal door of the suite startles me from my thoughts. Nadia's head snaps up with alarm and Tisis growls deep in her throat, moving to stand between the door and the little girl, fur on her back raised.

"Kelsey!" a muffled voice shouts from the hall. Jumping up, I fling open the door to find Rey, out of breath, cheeks red and fear etched across his face. Bandages cover his broken nose, both eyes are black with bruises and three stitches line his left cheekbone.

"Are you ok?" he demands, reaching out to clasp both my arms.

"What? Why wouldn't I be?"

Pushing past me, he does a frantic search of the suite. "Is anyone here with you?"

"Just Nadia," I say, motioning to the child. "And the wolf. Rey, what's wrong?"

"They're gone," he says between gasps for air as he faces me again. I notice the slight quiver in his hands as he lays his palms flat on the countertop and takes a deep inhale.

"Who's gone?"

"The League prisoners."

I inhale a sharp breath. "What? How? When?"

"I don't know... it's... I don't know."

"Did they escape or did Elijah..." my voice trails off because just the idea of him being here, in this building so close to everyone I love, I don't even want to think about it as terror slithers its icy fingers up my spine.

"I don't know. I just heard they were gone and ran to find you. I thought that, well, come on, everyone's down in the basement," he says and then hurries out the door to rush for the nearest stairwell.

"Nadia, stay here with Tisis, lock the door behind me and don't go anywhere!" I command. "And don't let anyone you don't know come in. Jax, Rey or I will find you once we're finished."

She's about to argue, her mouth open on a protest, but I pull the door shut and charge after Rey. Feet pounding on the linoleum and concrete, together we spiral down the stairs and into the basement where the Risers house prisoners or anyone else needing to be locked up. It should have only been the two League members down there.

The set-up is similar to the League's prison; old closets and storage rooms converted into crude cells with metal bars in place of doors. Old water and rust stains coat the grey cinder block walls, and dents, cracks and holes cover the concrete floor. The soles of my boots pound on the hard floor, reverberating through the vast space. We race past an ancient furnace no one has touched in the last century, and a collection of broken, rusted water heaters.

At the far end of the basement where an sold HVAC unit stands, holes rusted through the metal, we discover Charlie, Nole, Jax, Ryder and a handful of other people standing outside an empty cell with its metal grate pried open by force.

As the cell comes into view, I recoil with a yelp, colliding into Rey who pulls me against him.

He curses, trying to shield me from the ghastly sight inside the cell moments too late.

The two League prisoners are gone, but they haven't left

the cell empty. From a thick pipe running the length of the ceiling that must have once taken water through the building, hangs the body of a man. I recognize him from the crowd earlier, one of the Risers. A knife plunges through his chest, dried blood running down his clothes and pooling on the floor in a sickening, crimson puddle beneath his swaying feet. A braided rope cuts into his neck, the skin purple and grey and swollen. His eyes and tongue bulge from his face as he dangles and rotates on the end of the noose, arms drooped listlessly at his sides.

CHAPTER TEN

Hearing my yelp, the group turns towards where I cower in Rey's arms.

"Get her outta here!" barks Ryder, jabbing a thick finger at me.

Hands pull me away, I have no idea if they belong to Rey or someone else. All I can see is the man, swinging and bleeding. The stench of death chokes and gags me as I'm lead away, back up the stairs. Footsteps follow, the dull hum of voices buzzing in my ears.

As we reach the first floor, I'm guided to the *Resident Advisor's* office. The sound of weeping reaches my ears and glancing around a fresh gathering of people, I see Evy sobbing on another girl's shoulder. Charlie, Nole, Ryder and Jax file into the room behind me, everyone cramping together into the tight space, faces somber and pinched.

Shaking my head, trying to dispel the grotesque image, I fight to regain my composure. "What... what happened? How did they escape?"

"It would appear our prisoners were actually a ploy to figure out where you were hidin'," growls Ryder, shoulders tense and brow furrowed.

"Like I said when you first dragged them back here," a man replies. I recognize him as the one who first objected earlier when Ryder and I brought the League members back.

Ryder's head swivels around to catch the man in his venomous gaze.

"Don't start, Nathan," Nole warns. "Now isn't the time for a battle."

"Oh really? Cause one's here. Callum is dead, in case you missed the display downstairs. And it's his fault," the man snaps, stabbing a finger at Ryder. "It's all their faults. We were perfectly fine until they shows up begging for help for that Sub and now look!"

Ryder strides forward, a snicker on the edge of his lips and I recoil, remembering what he did to the League man and wondering how he'll react now.

"Silence, or leave, Nathan," orders Nole, stepping between the two men and thrusting a hand at the door.

Nathan arches a bushy eyebrow in challenge. "You'll turn your back on your own people? You'd rather protect a disgusting Sub than any of us?"

"Make your choice," snarls Nole with a menacing glower. Nathan glares, opening his mouth to respond, then changes his mind a marches for the hallway, flinging a pile of dusty books to the floor with a crash before making an inappropriate gesture with his right hand and slamming the door behind him.

Nole sighs. "He'll have the entire compound in an uproar within an hour."

"Right, then we figure out our next steps quickly," Charlie says.

I turn to her. "How did the League get in here in the first place?"

"They must have used those two as bait and planted additional spies to follow them upon capture. There was a metal exterior door to the basement which someone pried open with a crowbar and overtook our guards."

"How did they get past our patrols?" someone asks.

"No idea." She shakes her head and stares at the floor. "I hope we don't find more bodies of our men out in the woods come morning."

A long silence falls over our group with the exception of Evy's sobs, though I have no idea why she's crying. I wish she'd stop, the constant wailing sets me on edge.

Expecting someone to announce a plan, I look between Nole and Charlie. "Well, why don't we go after them? They have two injured League members, neither of whom looked like they would be ready for a long trek through the woods in their condition. They can't have made it that far."

Everyone in the group exchanges grim, helpless looks, as if they share a secret.

"It's not that simple," Charlie explains. "They took two of our men as hostages."

Puzzle pieces fall into place. I think I already know the answer to my next question, at least half of it anyway, but I need to hear it out loud. "Who did they take?"

Clearing his throat, Nole runs a hand through his hair. "One of my guards, Damian. And one of Charlie's."

I glance at Charlie and she nods, confirming my fears.

"They took Randolph."

Now I understand Evy's tears. My head spins and I place a hand against the cool, plaster wall to avoid crashing face-first to the floor. I feel like I've been punched in the stomach, my insides clenching and rolling. Rey takes my other arm, but I brush him away. This isn't the time to start a squabble between him and Jax, who stares at me so intently I'm uncomfortable even looking his direction.

"Hostages," I repeat warily, trying to assess the situation. "What do they want in exchange?"

This time everyone looks at the ground, even Rey and Jax, and it's Charlie and Nole who share a knowing glance.

"I guess we can't hid it from you anyway." Unfurling a piece of paper clenched in her fist, Charlie offers it to me. "They left this along with... along with the tip of a finger we believe belongs to Damian."

It's all I can do not to vomit. Blood coats the edges of the note, no doubt belonging to the dead Riser. I picture it pinned to his chest with the knife, a severed finger attached.

After a moment's hesitation, I take the paper between two trembling fingertips, careful to avoid any blood. Sliding the folds open, the League's demands are revealed.

I can't say I'm surprised, but seeing it in writing makes my knees weak and this time I slump against the wall, sliding to the floor until I sit on the cold, hard tile. Even as the words burn themselves into my memory, I'm unable to tear my eyes away from the scribbles on the paper.

Consider this a warning. If you don't want the same to happen to the two we have taken, Charlie must bring the Protector's daughter to your former compound by sundown tomorrow. No weapons. No guards. No games.

-Elijah

"You're not going," Jax says, his voice harsh. I'm so shocked he's actually spoken to me that I can only lift my head and stare dumbfounded. Rushing through the small throng of people, he kneels down and tears Elijah's note from my hand, crumples it into a ball and tosses it to the floor. Then, with the fingers of his good hand caressing the side of my face, his tone turns softer. "You aren't going."

"What?" Evy cries, still choking on sobs and yanking my attention away from Jax. Tears streak her cheeks. Her beautiful, shining hair hangs tangled and knotted around her shoulders and her eyes are so bloodshot they look like two red tomatoes stuck on her face. "They have my brother! They're going to kill him if we don't listen!"

"And you want to sacrifice Kelsey instead?" Jax demands, standing again, eyes blazing.

With pained features, Evy looks at me, clearly torn between saving her brother or saving me. "I... I want my brother..."

And suddenly everyone starts yelling at once. Some want me to go, some want me to stay, some want to attack the League again. Evy bawls. My head throbs as they all compete to see who can be louder in the tiny, echoing space.

"You read the note!" Evy screams, voice shrill with pain and hysteria. "They'll kill Randolph!"

"Someone please escort Miss Chung to her room," Charlie commands, unable to look at Evy's tear-stained cheeks and eyes so swollen they almost disappear into her face.

"No!" Evy shrieks, swatting at the girl who tries to draw her away. "I'm not going anywhere until I know how we're saving my bother! He's the only family I have left!"

"Well, we aren't sending Kelsey to the League for a third time to do it!" shouts Jax.

"Why the hell not?" another voice argues. "They're not gonna stop till they get the Sub! Heck, send 'em both."

"Why should we lose more lives for that girl?" another woman demands.

"Because we aren't animals," snaps a third voice. "We're not sending a young girl to be slaughtered. The League has been terrorizing us long before she showed up and they aren't going to stop even if they win now."

Slouching against the wall, I press my palms over my ears

in an attempt to drown out all the shouting. It does little good. I feel a hand on my knee and open my eyes to see Rey stooped before me, his blue eyes round with concern behind their bruises. "Kels, let's go back to your room."

"No," I say, trying to climb to my feet. Jax grabs one elbow and Rey the other to help until I shove them both away. "I'm not crippled! I can stand on my own!"

Everyone stops screaming for a moment to regard me with varying looks of concern and hatred and a wealth of mixed expressions in between.

"Actually, Miss Keslin, that might be a good idea," Nole says. "Charlie and I need to discuss this matter and how best to act to return everyone home safely. It would be best if those directly involved are perhaps not here for the debates."

I have no energy to argue, and Evy seems to be doing enough for the both of us as her jarring cries pierce my skull. I want to be angry at her for not caring what happens to me, but I can't really blame her. If I had to choose between Rey's safety or hers, I'd choose Rey's.

Of course, I'm unable to choose between Rey and Jax so maybe my opinion means little.

Both still hover beside me, Rey pulling my arm to lead me back to the stairs and Jax pushing a path through the crowded, suffocating room. Lost in my own thoughts, I slowly follow like a pitiful lost animal. My face burns as I feel every eye on me, far too many belonging to people who'd gladly stab me in the back if it meant they never had to see the League again.

"You should come back to stay with Nadia and me," Jax says as we get into the hallway, less a suggestion and more a plea.

"I don't know if that's a good idea," Rey grumbles as we trudge up the stairs.

"Well, of course you don't, I wouldn't expect a Sub-"

"Would you both just shut up!" I shriek, halting on the landing, my anger and frustration reaching full swell. "Just shut up and stop it! This is insane! A man died tonight because of me. Maybe even more. We have enough to worry about without the two of you acting like children fighting over a toy. I don't *belong* to either of you. I am not an inanimate object you get to control and if you both don't stop treating me like such I swear I might decide I hate both of you!"

My outburst is met with silence, Jax grounding his jaw to bite a sarcastic response, Rey hanging his head the way he always did when we were kids and I lost my temper with him. Neither response is typical for either boy when dealing with anyone other than myself. Somehow, whenever I'm concerned, they change, become more human or more caring or maybe more true to who they are, no longer hiding behind the masks they wear to protect themselves from the rest of the world.

With a deep inhale, I run my hands over my face, allowing my emotions to simmer. Jax and Rey aren't the ones I'm angry with right now. "I imagine if I say I'm going to stay in my own suite tonight, alone, you both are going to argue me to death about it?"

They glance at each other and then nod.

"And I also imagine that if I stay at Jax's, Rey will argue and vis-versa."

Both nod again. I pinch the bridge of my nose and sigh.

"Fine. Then we will all go to Jax's. I'll sleep with Nadia, Jax takes the other bedroom and Rey the couch in the common area. It'll be like one big, happy slumber party. Can we all deal with this scenario without fighting about it or punching anyone in the nose this time?"

"Yes," Rey says, looking relieved.

"Whatever," mutters Jax with a dispassionate shrug.

"Fine," I say, but only to gain some sort of last word so they know who's in charge. Then I head to my new suite to retrieve Nadia and the wolf. Regardless of the League and hostage situation, a very long night awaits us all.

CHAPTER ELEVEN

I can't sleep, which, given the course the evening took, isn't all that unforeseen. Every time I close my eyes I see the imagine of the hanging man. Every noise causes me to jump in fear that it might be Elijah.

Nadia snores gently, one thumb in her mouth and the blanket tucked up to her chin as she cocoons against my side. She wanted to know what happened and I hate to lie to her since she'll hear rumors anyway, but I didn't have the heart to tell her the full truth. I told her someone was killed, and two of our people kidnapped, but not about the note or Elijah's demands. She's dealt with more trauma than most adults could handle, it's time to start saving whatever innocence she has left.

Tisis lies at her feet, occasionally pricking her ears or lifting her head at some distant noise I'll never be able to hear. Her animal eyes appear to glow in the darkness.

My mind swirls with concern for Randolph, and even Damian, whom I've never even met, all combined with the fact that the League will never leave me alone until they have accomplished their mission. Or killed me. Or probably both. As long as Sawyer and Elijah walk this earth, I will never be safe and nor will those around me.

I know I have to follow Elijah's demands. If I don't, he'll kill Randolph and Damian and only come back for more. We're still outnumbered and out armed. What if he eventually kills Jax or Rey or Nadia? I can't bear the thought, but the idea of once again willingly surrendering myself to the League and whatever torture they have planned courses terror through my bones, causing me to shudder. After all the trouble I have caused them, they will kill me once I am no longer useful. And I can be sure it will be a slow, painful death at the psychotic hands of Elijah.

Dozens of plans form in my head and are quickly discarded because none of them will work. They might solve a temporary problem or save a life or two, but in the end they are nothing more than a Band-Aid on a gunshot wound. I'm sure Charlie and Nole are still awake downstairs with the same dilemma.

It must be well after midnight when I come to terms with what I have to do. No one will like it, in fact I hate it, but it's the only way. What choice do I have?

Slipping from bed, careful not to disturb Nadia, I tiptoe from the room, down the hall and to the front door. I'm nearly out of the apartment when a voice whispers through the darkness.

"Kelsey? Where are you going?"

It's Rey. Jax might sleep like a rock, but Rey never has and no matter how quiet I tried to be, he now sits up on the sofa, the shape of his tall, lanky body outlined in the moonlight through the common room windows.

"I can't sleep, I was going for a walk."

"Kels, you know I always know when you're lying right?"

Technically none of it was a lie, just an omission. I seem to be really good at those lately, though apparently not good enough to fool Rey.

"Where are you actually going?" he asks.

I chew my bottom lip. "To find Charlie and Nole so we can get Randolph and Damian back."

"Are you doing what I think you're doing?"

"Probably."

"Can I talk you out of it?"

"No."

"Then I'm coming with you," he says, rising to his feet. "And don't argue with me. You know I'll just follow whether you like it or not."

I snort. "Sometimes I wonder if you and Jax aren't the same person in two separate bodies. You both are ridiculously stubborn do an excellent job of driving me insane."

"Then that might explain why you love us both."

He doesn't say it with anger or intent to hurt, just the way one states a fact, the way Rey always exposes the obvious truth. It pains me anyway.

Rey places a firm hand on my shoulder and though I can't really see his face in the shadows of the room, I can picture his thin lips curved into a slight reassuring smile. "Hey, you'll always be my best friend, ok? Nothing will ever change that. Nothing."

I nod and smile as well, patting his hand with my own. "Nothing."

* * *

"Kelsey, you do understand what you're proposing?" Nole asks, his dark eyes rimmed with heavy circles and fine lines creased along his forehead. We found him and Charlie in the front office of the complex, candles burned low and both of them appearing exhausted as they gazed over a small mountain of illegible notes and free-handed diagrams meant to help them plan the best course of action.

"Yes, but it's really the only option we have."

"You know, this isn't actually what I thought you had planned," Rey says after remaining quiet the entire conversation. "But it might actually be better."

Nole leans forward, elbows resting on the table while he regards me carefully. "Kelsey, this is admirable, but-"

"But nothing. I'm the only one who can get close enough to Elijah and Sawyer to kill them."

"And you think you're capable of such?" Nole asks, thick eyebrows raised in question. "Killing two men?"

My throat compresses. "I've killed people before."

"In the heat of battle," Nole says. "This is different. This is a planned, calculated murder. I'm not saying it won't be justified, the world will be a better place without them, but you have to be one hundred percent certain that you're ready for this. There's no backing down or second guessing at the last minute."

I think of the League woman I stabbed to death to escape the first time. Nole doesn't know about that. It was planned murder as well. I did it for Nadia. And for Jax and Randolph too. I can do it now and maybe, someday, I can find a way to live with that decision.

"I have to be ready for this," I say. "We all know the only way this insanity with the League will end is with either their death or mine."

No one speaks. Even Rey, though I have no doubt a thousand objections charge through his mind.

"We have to admit she's right," Nole eventually says, meeting Charlie's gaze. "You said nearly the same thing about Sawyer an hour ago."

"I know," says Charlie her voice strained, the first words she's spoken since I presented my plan. She can't even look at me, choosing instead to stand and stare out of one of the windows. She looks exhausted, as like she has aged a decade in the last few hours, her gaze vacant. "But that doesn't make this the right choice. I don't see how one person can kill two people, plus getting around whatever guards they'll have protecting them, and still survive."

"Maybe I was never meant to survive," I whisper. Now every eye darts toward me, looks of distress across their faces.

"Kelsey-" Rey says with horror before I cut him off.

"Maybe I wasn't. Maybe the only way this ends and the only way the people I care about are safe, is if all three of us are dead."

And I mean it. Regardless of the outcome, my plan is the only one guaranteed to work because in the end, someone will die and this will be over.

"There has to be another way," Charlie says, her face fallen and sorrowful as she glances to Nole for hope. "I am not taking her there alone and leaving her to suffer at the hands of Sawyer himself. Who knows what he'll do. I cannot allow this to become a suicide mission."

Nole sits deep in thought, arms folded over his chest and coal black eyes gleaming in the lantern light, though he appears miles away. He sits like this for nearly a full minute as we all watch him, waiting for a solution.

"Maybe there is. Charlie, come with me. Kelsey, get some rest and be prepared to leave tomorrow."

"Wait, can't I-"

"Nope," he says, marching to the door and ushering Rey and I back into the hallway before gesturing for Charlie to follow him.

Whatever their plan, I will not be privy to the details. Not exactly my choice, but Nole's mind is made up.

"I still think this is totally nuts," Rey says as Nole and Charlie disappear into the depths of the building. "Even with whatever Nole's idea is."

Rey and I tromp back to Jax's apartment to catch a few more hours of sleep. Or whoever's apartment it now belongs to with four people and one wolf living there. Given the space constraints, it's almost like being back in ROC.

"Like, this is more insane than you kidnapping Wyatt Walker at gun point and choosing death by radiation, and that was certifiably nuts," he says. "Nuts, ok?"

"Your opinions have been noted and I'm still going," I reply, jaw set in determination as I march up the stairs ahead of him.

"I have no doubt, but I wish you'd let me talk you out of it."

"Going where?" a suspicious voice asks and I glance up the last flight to see Jax enter from the third floor hall. With disheveled hair and rumbled clothes, I'm guessing he just woke up and discovered Rey and me missing.

I never intended to keep my plan a secret from Jax, but I wanted to prepare how best to tell him. Now we both stand at opposite ends of the staircase while he quickly puts two-and-two together.

He rubs the bridge of his nose and groans.

"Please, please tell me you are not handing yourself to the League?" he demands, arms crossed and eyes narrowed. "Again. This is getting old."

I immediately go on the defensive. "It's not like last time. Nole and Charlie have a plan. We're going to kill Elijah and Sawyer and end this."

"That doesn't answer my question."

"She's going," Rey says with forceful distaste, allowing the words to hang in the air like the poisonous gas of the ROC chambers.

Jax's face morphs into a deep scowl. "Just how many times are you going to march into the League's hands? Haven't we already seen how this ends?"

"I'm going to do it as many times as it takes for the people I care about to be safe. They're only doing this because of me. And this time will end differently because not only are they expecting me, but we're going in on the offensive rather than the defensive."

"And you're ok with that?" Jax growls, jerking his heated gaze to Rey.

Rey shrugs and shakes his floppy blond hair. "No, I'm seriously pissed about it actually. But it's Kelsey. I'm sure you know by now that she's going to do whatever she thinks is best and no one can stop her."

Then Rey stomps up the last few steps, brushes past Jax and vanishes into the hall leaving Jax and I to stare at each other in uncomfortable silence like two enemies on opposing lines of battle.

"It's a good plan," I finally say, though it sounds significantly less confident out loud than in my head. "I think. I mean, Nole and Charlie are smart. Whatever they're planning, I'm sure it'll work. And I won't be alone." I add hurriedly.

"You don't even *know* the full plan?"

"Nole and Charlie and putting it together now. It's Nole's idea really. He said I didn't need to know the details, but I trust him. I'm sure you trust him too."

Jax appears unconvinced, his jaw grinding. Then he treks down the stairs toward me. It makes no sense, but I think he's going to try to kiss me. Or maybe push me or yell or something. Instead he storms past and continues down the stairwell.

"Jax!"

He whips around and for a moment, the pain in his eyes

so evident it cuts into my heart.

"As Rey just said," Jax spits, "you do what you want and no one can stop you. Not even those your decisions will hurt most. Go. Stay. I don't care anymore."

Then he's vanished around the bend in the stairwell, his footsteps banging down the final steps below before another door slams shut.

"I'm doing this to protect the people I care about most!" I scream, but he's long gone. Furious and frustrated, I collapse onto the nearest step and drop my head into my hands.

I have to go. I have to. I will not let others die because of me. Besides, this is our chance, possibly our *only* chance to destroy the League for good. Doesn't that outweigh my feelings? And Jax and Rey's too? It's not like my death is guaranteed. Nole seemed convinced, or at least as much as anyone can be all things considered. There's a chance I might survive yet again, if my luck hasn't completely run out.

"Kelsey?" a tiny voice whispers. At first, I think it's Nadia, but when I look up, Evy stands before me, nervously shifting from one barefoot to the other. She looks awful with red-rimmed eyes, a puffy face and limp, tangled hair. She twists her hands around each other and sniffles a couple times.

"Evy," I say with surprise, having been too caught up in myself to hear her approach. Then my stomach sinks because I think she's going to yell or sob again and I'm in no mood to handle either. "Look, I don't think-"

"No. I'm not... I'm not here to..." She takes a deep breath and then her next words flow out so quickly I have a hard time keeping up. "I just wanted to tell you I'm sorry. Charlie just found me and told me what you've agreed to do and I... I'm thankful you're going to save Randolph, but I don't want anything bad to happen to you either. I acted like a jerk last night. You're my friend and I care about you too, I just... I-" and she begins to cry again, tears running down her already stained, swollen cheeks.

"Evy," I say again, standing to put a supportive arm around her as she flops against me. "Everything is going to be ok. We'll get your brother back. Damian too. And I'll be ok." The words are meant to comfort me as much as Evy.

"I know," she says with a sniffle. "I'm just so scared for everyone. Ugh, I can't stop crying even though my eyes and head and face hurt so bad. I must look like a lunatic." Wiping at her cheeks, she laughs a little. Which then makes me laugh and then for some reason we are both laughing so hard we have to sit, still clutching at each other as we sink to the steps, our bodies pressed together in the tight space between the wall and the railing.

"This is awful. Why are we even laughing?" she asks, catching her breath.

"I have no idea, but what else are we going to do right now?"

"I passed Jax on my way up. He looked really upset. I'm guessing he's not as on board with this plan as Charlie and Nole?"

Pursing my lips, I turn my gaze to the floor and run a hand through the knots in my hair. "I don't know what to do with Jax. He... I don't know."

"You like him right?"

"Yes."

"The sun is coming up and you'll need to leave soon. You really should go talk to him. You know, just in case."

I know she's right. I should talk to him, if only to make sure I don't march into the League's grasp without having to worry about how I've left things between us.

"I don't know where he went," I say instead.

"He likes water," Evy replies. "There's a little river behind the last building past the fields, the one with only three walls. If you walk along the edge of the trees, you'll find the path. I'd bet that's where he went."

Rising, I brush my palms against my jeans. "Thanks, Evy."

"Yeah," she says as I turn to head down the stairs.

"Hey, Kelsey? Be careful today, ok? I want Randolph to come home, but I want you to come home too."

Home. That's what this has become. I've been here a month and it already feels more like a home, like my home, than ROC ever did. I smile. "Of course I will. With that goofy looking brother of yours in tow."

CHAPTER TWELVE

Exiting the building, I see the first hints of sunlight on the grey horizon, a haze of fresh humidity floating before it. A breeze brushes through the waist-high grass, causing the tips of it to tickle my fingertips. In inhale deeply, loving the smell of fresh air and pine trees. Birds chip from the trees and the last of the crickets are settling down for a new day.

Following Evy's directions, I round the last building in the complex, duck through an opening in the trees, follow the path for a minute or so and there he is, sitting alone on a large mossy hunk of cement staring at a narrow, trickling river that flows through the trees. It bubbles and gurgles, spilling over small rocks on its journey.

As I approach, Jax turns at the sound of my footsteps and for a second I'm worried he'll be mad, or whatever he's been since Rey came back.

He says nothing though, turning his attention back to the water and ignoring me as I stand awkwardly beside the cement boulder, shuffling my feet in the damp dirt and dewy grass.

"Hey," I finally say because I can't handle the tension anymore.

"Hi," he says, but doesn't look at me, paving the way for more heavy silence that crushes down on my shoulders.

"I'm sorry you're upset about me going today, but it needs to be done."

"That's not really why I'm upset."

"Then why?"

He offers one of his noncommittal shrugs that means absolutely nothing to me other than Jax not wanting to display any actual feelings or emotions. God forbid he admit he's human.

"Is this really how you want it to be now?" I ask angrily. "Barely speaking to each other?"

He shrugs again, still observing the water. I wonder if he feels like he's back at his spot overlooking the massive lake near the compound. I find myself missing it and wonder if he does too. After all, it had been his sole place of reflective solitude. Now he's lost that too.

Thinking of the beautiful turquoise water, I'm reminded once again how his eyes and his lake are the same color and yet nothing alike at all. The water in the lake always flowed calm and peaceful and serene, but Jax's eyes hide a turmoil and fear that runs so deep, I'm not even sure he is aware. How can two things that look almost identical on first glance, be so very different beneath the surface?

"I thought you might need space to sort things out," he says. "Figure out what you want when it comes to Rey and me. I don't suppose, given what might happen later today, that you've decided to pick one of us and that's why you've come here to bother me?"

A whoosh of air rushes out of my lungs like a deflating balloon. His words hurt, but they are true. "No, that's not why I came. I wanted us to at least be ok before I left, just in the chance things don't go well."

"Does it matter?"

"So this is how it's going to be between us?" I demand in frustration, kicking at the ground when I really just want to push him off the cement slab and into the water. "We can't even be friends?"

Now he looks at me, his face sharp and serious. "I told you I wanted to be more than friends."

"So that's it then? It's all or nothing with you?"

"It's not like *you* know what you want it to be!"

"That's not fair. Why do you have to be such a jerk just because I'm confused? Why can't we at least be friends and just see what happens?"

"It's not that simple."

"Well, it doesn't need to be this complicated either!"

"I love you!" he shouts, his perfect features a twisted mask of pain and disbelief, as if he can't fathom how I don't see how much he loves me. The thing is, I do see. I see it in his eyes every time he looks at me, I just haven't been brave enough to acknowledge it.

Seeing how much I've hurt him only makes me hurt worse, a gunshot through my heart. I've known he loves me. He hasn't actually said it before, but that much has been undeniably obvious and now, the first time he's said it has been from anger and agony, both of which I've caused.

His features soften, regaining their composure, as though he'd never lost it in the first place, the stoic lake surface returning once more to hide the turmoil beneath.

"I love you, Kelsey. I tried to tell you that night under the fireworks, but then Rey came back and everything changed and it wasn't the right time anymore. I want you to be happy, preferably with me, but if you choose Rey that's fine as long as it's what you want. But I can't sit in this limbo of what-ifs and maybes, daring to hope that you might choose me. Especially knowing that you might... that after tonight there's a possibility I never see you again."

It's a long time before either of us speaks. Knees bent, arms circling his legs, Jax has returned to watching the water, though I don't think he actually sees it. I scuff my boots in the mud trying to make sense of thoughts and emotions that hold none.

"I'm climbing up on that rock Jax, and I'm going to sit beside you." I don't know why I feel a need to announce it. Maybe I'm worried if I don't warn him first, he'll shove me back off.

"Do whatever you want."

Hesitantly, I pull myself onto the damp moss until I sit less than two inches from him, though the space feels like miles. I wonder, regardless of whatever choice I make, if we will ever be able to eliminate that distance again. I've driven a wedge between us and time has morphed it into a canyon and I might never be able to fix the damage I've done.

"Jax," I say carefully, as if I am talking to a wild animal that might attack. "I... I care about you. I do. You mean the world to me and if Rey hadn't come back, it would be us together. But he did, and he means everything to me too. I care about both of you more than I care about myself, that's why this is so hard. I just... I need time, even if I maybe don't have any. I'm sorry. I really am. I wish I could give you more than that, I just can't right now."

Shifting so he faces me, Jax's eyes meet mine for the first time in days. My heart beats too fast and my breath quickens as he stares into my face. "Do you love me?"

I hang my head. "Jax-"

"Please, Kelsey. I need to know. I know you love Rey, I can accept that, but do you love me too?"

Suddenly I want to look anywhere but at Jax, averting my gaze until it darts over the rock, over the ground, over the water. Yet in the end, I turn back to him, unable to fight the urge to see his beautiful features; the sharp angle of his jaw, the graceful curve of his lips. Those eyes.

"I do," I say softly, my insides melting with affection. "I love you too."

I can feel the callouses and scars covering both his hands as he places them on my cheeks. Then he leans forward and kisses me and we fold into each other. My face flushes as I draw in a deep breath because even though it's only been a matter of days since we last kissed, it somehow feels like months have passed instead.

Enveloping me into an embrace, his arms strong yet tender as they wrap around my body, Jax lowers me down until I lie on the rock and he hovers over me, propped on one elbow. His other hand glides across my hipbone and his fingertips slide under the hem of my shirt. They're hot against my stomach. Their warm caress trails down my side and slips under my lower back, pressing me closer to him. Goose bumps rise along my skin.

He kisses me again, hungry and passionate. I know I should stop him, push him away because this isn't fair; not to Rey who I still love and certainly not to Jax who I am now misleading... or whatever awful thing I'm doing. But I am selfish and terrible and instead I reach up to pull his face harder against mine because I can't get enough of him. Like a drug, I need more, and whatever happens from here, I want to remember this moment forever.

Breaking away, he kisses along my jaw and down my neck and I shiver from the gentle touch. Like feathers, his lips brush along my collar bone and all I can do is cling to the back of his shirt with my fingers.

Resting the side of his face on my shoulder, I'm certain he can hear my heart beating quick and forcefully. Neither of us move as we lay there holding each other, the warmth of the rising sun beaming down, though its heat can never compare to ours.

"I'm glad you came," he whispers.

"I thought you wanted to be alone."

Sitting up, he stares down at me. With the golden edges of the sun backlighting his features, it looks like a halo around his head; a dark angel floating above me. All he needs is wings.

Without thinking, I reach up and trace the line of his cheekbone with my fingertips. He catches my hand in his own, holding it to his face as if he draws some sort of energy from me.

"Not just today I mean," Jax corrects. "I meant up here, coming out of ROC and into my world. Something was missing, it's always been missing for as long as I can remember, I just never knew what it was until now."

He looks so vulnerable all of a sudden and I know how hard it was for him to admit that. I am reminded of the promise I made Daniel that I would never hurt Jax. That for as strong as he is, he is also cracked somewhere inside, like a glass, and one tiny vibration might cause him to shatter into a million pieces never to be whole again. Daniel was so afraid Jax would break and needed me to keep him together. It was his dying request.

And yet I am, hurting Jax anyway. Every second that passes with me unable to choose drives a knife deeper into his heart; and one deeper into Rey's and another into mine until it is very possible none of us will survive anyway.

CHAPTER THIRTEEN

As I emerge from the school onto the front steps several hours later, I'm just in time to witness a group of sixty or so people hiking into the woods. Packs of food and canteens of water are slung over their backs. Some carry weapons, but none look ready for battle. I see Raoul and his wife and daughter among them. Other children as well. And the man, Nathan, who was so outspoken last night.

"Are they part of the plan?" I ask Charlie, stepping up beside her.

"No. They're leaving."

"Leaving what?"

"Us. The compound. The Risers. They're going to make their own group elsewhere."

She's so stoic, as if they're just field workers meandering off to start their day, not her friends, people she has lead for however many years, now deserting her when we need every person we can get.

"How?" I demand, anger unfurling. "Why?"

"They don't agree with the choices Nole and I have made. It's ok, Kelsey. They are welcome to leave. We encouraged it and sent them with enough supplies to last a couple weeks until they can get themselves settled down with another group or build a compound of their own. It's that or they stay here and add to the tension and animosity."

"But how can they just *leave*?"

She turns to me. "They aren't prisoners here. People come and go all the time. They don't agree with mine and Nole's decisions, they are unhappy, so they have chosen to move on. I cannot fault people for doing what they believe is best for themselves or their families."

My mouth hangs open as I watch the group vanish into the trees and underbrush of the forest. I should be happy Raoul is gone, one less person around here who wants me dead, but I can't help but feel guilty. I'm the reason they feel they must leave their home. I'm the reason the surface groups are falling apart.

"You ready?" Charlie asks. "We have about five hours to sundown."

"Yeah," I say reluctantly, a giant lie. I tuck my fresh t-shirt into my jeans and twist my hair back up before turning my attention to her, trying to move past the members that have departed. She gives a grim smile.

"Good. Neither am I."

Her honest response puts a tiny grin on my own lips, easing some of my anxiety and making me thankful I'm not alone. A moment later, Nole and several other Risers and compound members exit the complex as well to give us a final send off into whatever fate has in store. Nole offers us both flasks of water and small packs of food.

"Everyone is set," he says, reaching out to rest a hand on each of our shoulders. At least someone has confidence.

"Anything I should know?" I ask nervously because I still have no idea what the full plan is.

"No," he says. "Just do as Elijah's note instructed."

Both Charlie and I nod before turning to walk away, leaving the others behind us because Elijah's note told us to come alone. I trust the mysterious plan and the people involved, but it still doesn't allay my fear or end the gnawing sense of panic and dread in my gut. Whatever has been decided, there's so many ways this can go wrong and I can't stop thinking about Jax and everything he said earlier. I almost wish I hadn't made an effort to leave with us on good terms. If he were still mad at me, it might make this easier, I could use the flames of fury to my advantage. Now I'm weighted with fear.

"I'm scared too," Charlie says, as if reading my thoughts.

"Really? You hardly ever show it."

"I've had more practice at hiding my emotions than you have."

"I'd rather not be afraid at all instead of having to hide it," I grumble.

"I don't. It means we're human and we're alive. Those with no fear... like Elijah or Sawyer... it means there's something wrong with them. Like they're missing an essential part. Besides, courage can't exist without fear to create it. The two go hand-in-hand."

I suppose she's right. If I'm scared, it means I'm human and if I'm human it means I can't be a monster despite what I intend to accomplish tonight, who I might kill before the next sunrise. I only hope I can hold on to that part of myself when this is over.

We've reached the edge of the tree line and I pause to glance back at the apartment complex where Nole and the others stand to watch us leave.

"Everything ok?" Charlie asks and I nod, not wanting to tell her that I wanted to see Rey and Jax once more. I have no idea where they've gone and I'm disappointed they didn't come to see me off. At least Rey. I can't believe he didn't come.

My gut twists because I shouldn't want to see either of them until I have made a decision and the fact that I am headed forward with this mission without ever deciding makes me feel worse. Maybe I should hope for my death, it will make things a whole lot easier. Dead people don't have to pick who they love more. Dead people don't have to do much of anything really.

Ducking into the trees, the shadows of the forest pass over both of us, though do little to quell the heavy humidity in the air. It must be mid-May by now. I've missed Elsa's employment anniversary, and wonder, for the millionth time, if she's alright, what happened to her after I disappeared.

I suppose I have far bigger things to worry about though.

* * *

The woods have entered the first stages of twilight and we're less than a mile from Charlie's former compound when two League members emerge from the shadows, frightening me. Both are clad in full combat gear including their giant helmets, concealing their faces in the growing darkness. Their guns are raised to point at our chests. It almost makes me laugh, the extremes they've gone through for two unarmed women.

I can't say I expected a different greeting though, certainly no flower bouquets or warm hugs, but still my heart leaps into my throat as my hands jump into the air in defense. I know they won't shoot me, I'm too important to Sawyer's cause, but I'm scared for Charlie. Why else would Elijah demand her presence except to make an example out of her? To punish her for what the Risers and her compound have done to the League? Or maybe to use her to force me to comply? I can only hope Nole's plan works before anything happens to her. I can't handle watching Charlie die the same way I watched Daniel. Or even Ashlynn. Or that man all those years ago the day of the Gamble, shot and killed outside my suite's door. How many deaths have I witnessed at this point? I don't want to think about it. That number *should* be zero.

One League man steps forward, drawing several lengths

of rope which he uses to bind both mine and Charlie's hands behind our backs. Then, with pokes from the barrels of their guns, we are herded though the woods until we reach the walls of Charlie's compound. I can't see beyond the barbed-wire topped stone, but black soot mars the rocks and mortar, scorched in some places from the flames that destroyed the compound. The air still carries a faint smell of smoke and charred wood. I know that nothing but smoldering ruins lie behind the barricade that once offered me protection and a sense of comfort. For just a short period of time, it had been my home.

Now everything is gone and I wish I could cry for what has been lost, but I won't. Like when I believed my friends were dead, I won't give Elijah the satisfaction of thinking he's broken me. He won't break me. I won't allow it.

Beside the entrance, Elijah waits with more of his men, all fanned around him like a giant halo. Even in the dim light, I can see the wickedness burning in his face.

"I have to say, I didn't think you'd follow my orders."

"We want our two men released," Charlie says. "Kelsey and I will go with you without a fight once we know they are safe."

He smirks, white teeth gleaming in the rise of the silver moonlight. "Considering you are both well out-numbered, have no weapons and have your hands tied, I'm not sure how you think you have any negotiating power."

"Where are Randolph and Damian?" Charlie demands, completely ignoring Elijah's verbal jabs. He clenches his jaw before nodding his head to the man beside him. The man sticks two fingers in his mouth and whistles. A few moments later, Randolph and a middle- aged man with a barrel chest, round face and balding head are lead from the trees. Both are bound and gagged and escorted by multiple armed guards. Even in the darkness, I can see they have been beaten; bruises patterning their faces. Randolph walks with a heavy limp.

"Let them go," Charlie commands again and even though she is in no position to dictate, she still appears powerful and strong, her face a mask of defiance and I am proud to stand beside her in what could well be our final moments.

Elijah smiles one of his cold inhuman smiles, all teeth and no warmth or emotion.

"No," I whisper in horror as a terrifying thought comes over me, but my voice is so soft no one hears. My throat tightens, a lump forming as panic unfurls beneath my ribs, gripping my heart. I've been here before. I know what will happen next.

"No!" I cry louder, but I am too late as the League guards with Damien and Randolph lift their weapons, preparing to shoot their captives.

Time slows down as the world around me speeds up. All I can picture in my mind were the seven ROC citizens murdered in Sawyer's mall. The seven people that were supposed to be freed because of me. I suppose they are free in a way, but death is never the freedom I would have chosen for them. And now I will watch it happen again.

I try to lunge forward, for all the good it will do anyone, but strong hands fling me aside. I topple to the hard earth, pain shooting through my shoulder and my head smacks the ground leaving me dizzy and disoriented. Charlie lies next to me, though I have no idea how she ended up on the ground too.

Shots fire, the sounds ringing in my ears. I struggle against my bonds and flop to twist around, wanting to see if Randolph is really dead, but then not wanting to see at all. If I don't see it, maybe it never happened, I'll never have to pollute my mind with the image of one more dead body.

"Kelsey!" Charlie hisses. "Stay down!"

I lift my eyes to find hers. Despite all the chaos of battle around us, she remains unruffled and focused.

"But Randolph," I say, the words coming out as sobs. I wasn't even aware I was crying.

"They'll be ok," she replies. "Please, just trust me."

I want to yell about how she can't possibly believe that. They are dead, I am sure of it, and soon we will be too. No one will be ok.

Gunfire erupts around me, shots from every direction and I have no idea who's even shooting at whom. There are shouted commands and screams of pain and the sound of bodies hitting the earth with pierced yelps from the dying. One body lands on top of me and I squeeze my eyes shut, trying not to move and ignore the fact that the dying man's blood drips onto my neck, warm and sticky. He gasps for air, a gurgling sound emanating from the back of his throat before he stops breathing all together.

Charlie keeps murmuring that it will all be ok. I no longer know if she's saying it to convince me, or to convince herself.

And as quickly as it all began, less than ninety seconds later, it's over. A few moments of hush fill the forest, interrupted only by the deep, ragged breathing of those who have survived the sudden battle. I continue to remain motionless, half trapped between the ground and the dead body. All I can think about is Randolph, wondering if he's managed to survive. What will I tell Evy if we don't bring her brother home alive? I can't see Charlie anymore and hope she's safe as well... and what exactly just happened anyway?

The weight of the corpse lifts off me, allowing for my lungs to expand with a full breath. I taste remnants of gunpowder that linger in the air like bits of dust, followed by the metallic tinge of spilt blood. I spit and sputter to get the tastes from my mouth.

Someone picks me up and places me on my feet. I turn to find one of the League members; the man's full body armor and helmet having saved him from any bullets.

The weight of despair crushes down as though another dead body had been flung over me. For a moment, I had thought that maybe Charlie and I were saved, that whatever Nole's plan was had actually worked.

Aiming his gun at my feet, the League member unhooks his helmet and lifts it from his head. My mouth falls open in shock as the man smiles.

"Hey, poppet. How's it goin'?"

CHAPTER FOURTEEN

"What…" I begin before my voice trails off because I have no idea what I wanted to say in the first place. I take in the scene before me as all of the helmeted League members remove the masks concealing their faces. Ivan, Nole, even a woman whose name I don't know but I recognize her as a Riser. Lara is there too and four others I don't recognize, but who seem to be on our side because they aren't shooting anyone.

Scattered around the small clearing are bodies of the actual League members, all dead, some before they could even pull their weapons.

As my eyes dart around, they come to rest on a figure kneeling before Lara. She holds a gun to his flame-red hair. Though he doesn't move, and I'm sure he'd be shot the moment he did, I can't help but feel the familiar fear unravel through me.

"You decided to save *him*?" I demand, my tone far nastier than I intended as my eyes narrow and teeth grind together.

"That one," Ryder responds, stalking forward to grab Elijah's hair, wrenching the man's face upward. "Is our ticket to Sawyer."

I turn to Charlie in time to see Nole slip a knife from his belt and slice the ropes binding her hands. He takes a moment to pull her hair back over her shoulder and whisper something in her ear causing her to smile sweetly and squeeze his hand. Then she glances at Elijah and her smile falls, her face distorting into something else entirely.

I return my attention to Ryder, whose dark eyes sparkle

from the excitement of winning the battle.

"I don't understand," I say, as the rock of a man cuts the ropes around my own wrists, setting me free. I edge away from him.

"You think we were just gonna let you and Charlie prance into League hands?" Ryder asks, a huge grin covering his face, as if it's the funniest idea he's ever heard. "Come on, surely you think better of me by now?"

I'm not really sure what I think of Ryder anymore. But that's an internal debate for another day.

"Where did you get the uniforms? And how?"

Dried leaves and dead grass crunch and a second later Nole stands beside me. "I've had them for years. My men have been taking them off dead League members and hiding the bodies any chance they got. I've been saving them for a special occasion, so to speak. The best way to infiltrate the enemy is to trick them into believing you are a friend. I had our team put on the uniforms and then wait for the League to appear and find a creative way to switch places."

"Switch places?" I ask. "What is that supposed to mean?"

"You really wanna know?" Ryder asks, bushy eyebrows lifted in question.

No. I don't want to know. After his display the other night, I can imagine. I suppose it doesn't matter. Once again, and despite all odds, I am safe and one step closer to my mission. Glancing around, I see Randolph and Damian a few paces away, wide eyed but alive as one of the Risers checks them over and cuts off their own bindings.

"Let's just go," I say, glancing at Elijah who offers a disgusted sneer. I want to barge over and punch him in the face and then hit him again and again until that filthy smile is gone for good. My hands ball into fists, fingernails digging into my palms until they sting, but right now, we need him.

"You heard the lady!" Nole shouts, circling one finger in the air. "Randolph and Damian, you're both headed back home with some of our guards. As for everyone else, you know the plan so let's haul out."

Heaving Elijah to his feet, Ryder, Lara and Ivan trail him with their weapons.

"Don't go thinkin' we won't shoot you if you try anythin' funny," Ryder announces. "We can certainly use you right now, but we got plenty of backup plans if I decide your face looks better with a bullet hole. You got me?"

Elijah nods, his jaw clenched so tight his temples pulse with fury. Shoving him forward, our team moves through the forest in the direction of the League's mall, or whatever is left of it after Jax's fireworks display. I have to admit, I'm kind of excited to see what damage we caused. Once all this is over, I want to see the entire thing ablaze a second time. Leave it as nothing more than a pile of burning ash like they did to Charlie's compound. Seems fair.

Nole tromps ahead, black hair shining as he leads the team. I jog forward and fall into step beside him. "So, what is the rest of the plan?"

"What do you mean?" he asks, his tone falsely innocent.

"I mean, even with Elijah hostage, a dozen of us aren't going to be much of a match against whatever League members are left. Are there more coming?"

"Of course."

"Is… are… are Jax and Rey…"

Nole stops so suddenly I walk two more steps before coming to a halt as well, flipping around to face him. The others walk past without so much as a second look and he waits, taking several long moments before responding.

"I'm going to tell you the same thing I told both of them when they showed up at pounding on my door at sunrise. Together, I should add, because apparently when they're arguing the same case, they are a united front. If we are going to be successful, you need to have your head in the game, and that means that you can't be worried about what happens to others."

"But they're my... friends," I say because I have no idea what to call either of them at this point.

"And mine, as are all of the others involved. But this is a war. Hopefully the end of a war, but a war just the same. You have to learn to compartmentalize and shut out anything that might interfere with your thinking or your emotions or your logic. I've learned how to do it. Charlie learned how to do it. If you're going to be the kind of leader I think you can become, you need to learn how to do it as well. That's how you survive and how the greater good of your people survive. We are going to lose people today, that is inevitable, and there will be a time for mourning and grief and tears, but not until we have won. Figure out how to remove Jax and Rey from your thoughts tonight, or say behind. I don't want someone on the battlefield if they aren't one hundred percent focused on the mission because that person is no longer a soldier, they are a liability."

He stalks away as I stand dumbfounded in the middle of the woods, my mouth hinged open like a cracked door. I don't move for several seconds, Nole's statement swirling through my thoughts.

I suppose he's right. I can't go into this worrying about Rey or Jax or anyone else. It's mostly my fault we're all in this mess anyway.

Not wanting to be left in the dark woods that may or may not contain more League members, I quicken my pace and fall into step with Charlie.

"You knew all about this?" I ask.

"Of course. We set it up together."

"No one felt a need to tell me even part of it? Could have made me feel a lot better when we left."

"No. You didn't need to know. The fewer people who did, the better. The others coming behind us don't even know. It's best when not everyone has the full information, just in case."

"Because we don't know who to trust?" I ask thinking of Ashlynn and her betrayal.

"Yes, but also in case any of our team is captured. I'm sure you've noticed by now that Elijah and Sawyer have no problems with inflicting harm just because they can. I can only imagine what they would do if someone had information they wanted.

"And yet Sawyer is so focused on everyone using 'please' and 'thank you'," I grumble. "His priorities are seriously out of whack."

She sighs, licking her bottom lip. "He's always been like that. Always operated on a broken moral compass guided by insane ideals."

My nose wrinkles and I squint at her in the dark. "How do you know?"

"I've been in this game a long time."

For several minutes we walk side by side trailing along behind the lantern-light of the others ahead of us. I can see it glint off Elijah's vibrant hair as he shuffles between Ryder and Ivan, both of whom march with long, straight backs, shoulders wide and heads held high. Like father, like son.

"I guess life on the surface isn't all that different from inside ROC," I say.

"What do you mean?"

"At the end of the day, everyone is just trying to survive."

"Congratulations. You've summed up all of human history in one sentence."

"But doesn't that make you depressed? Shouldn't life be more than just surviving? Shouldn't it be better than that?"

"It can be, but it's on you to achieve it. No one will hand 'better' to you. It will never be easy and sometimes you have to fight to the death for it. Most people are too afraid to do so. Or they've allowed themselves to be lead to believe it doesn't work that way. They're wrong."

"That's what we're doing tonight then? Fighting for our chance at more than just survival?"

She offers a sly smile. "Of course it is. Why else would we be doing this?"

"All right, listen up," Nole calls, bringing everyone to a stop as we form a small circle. "We're about a quarter mile from the League's patrolled perimeter. Once we cross into their lines, we'll have another mile and a half until we hit whatever is left of their mall and then need to get through the still standing portion of the building to Sawyer, all without anyone realizing the little change-up in pecking order tonight." He jerks his head toward Elijah, who responds with a cold sneer and flaring nostrils.

"Unfortunately," Nole continues, "Charlie and Kelsey, this means we need to tie you up again."

I blink in surprise. "Wait, what? Why?"

"Cause part of our plan is to make it look like Elijah was successful in his," Nole replies.

"Our version of hidin' in plain sight," Ryder announces with a chuckle. "Turnin' the League's game right back around at them."

I point to Elijah. "But then that means we have to untie him."

"Yeah," Ryder says, jabbing at Elijah with his gun, "but I think our dear friend understands that if he says or tries anythin', literally anythin' at all, I'll shoot him in a heartbeat."

"And how do I know you won't just shoot me anyway once you get whatever it is you all want?"

"If you'd like, I can shoot ya now and be done with it?" Ryder asks, his face dark and serious and I can't help but shiver at his ominous tone because I know he's serious. Elijah emits an angry snort, but clenches his mouth shut.

"Thought so," Ryder says.

"I apologize, Kelsey," Nole says, "but this is all necessary. Can you trust me right now?"

I do trust him, and Charlie and everyone else that stands in our little circle, except Elijah of course. But the thought of having my hands bound while the man who has beaten, drugged and tried to kill me several times won't be tied up, leaves me with a mounting sense of unease and foreboding. But I don't see any other way around it. Whatever Nole planned, it's all worked well so far.

"Sorry little poppet," Ryder says as Lara steps forward to knot fresh rope around my wrists. She's gentle as she can be, but it has to be believable so the rope chaffs and rubs painfully at my already raw skin.

"Any chance I can at least get a gun?"

"Got one right here for you," Nole announces, patting a holster attached to the waist of his League uniform. "And a good, sharp knife. You'll get it soon as possible."

It makes me feel a little better as I watch Charlie bound as well. Then Nole cuts off Elijah's bindings. "We're serious about shooting you. If I think for a second you're going to compromise our mission, I'll drive the bullet through your forehead myself."

Rubbing at his wrists, Elijah flashes a nasty glower. "Whatever."

My team re-dons their helmets and facemasks and moments later, I am once again a prisoner of the League.

CHAPTER FIFTEEN

I hate that I have my hands tied and that I continue to be unarmed the closer we travel to League headquarters. Twice I ask Nole if I can at least have a knife.

"What for?" he asks after my second request. "I'm here. You've got nothing to worry about."

I consider pointing out that Rey said the same thing to me the night before the Gamble which started this entire fiasco, but I keep my mouth shut. I don't need a reminder of the past, especially right now. Besides, while it's unlikely Elijah will live to see the morning, I still don't want him to know about Rey. It's the only protection I can offer my best friend.

I peek at Elijah from the corner of my eye, Ryder's lantern light falling on the man's freckled face. He shows no fear, not so much as the slightest concern for his dire situation and I think of my conversation earlier with Charlie, how he's missing something essential to being human. Surely he must know his odds aren't good. Even if we don't win tonight, there's no way Nole or Charlie or Ryder will let Elijah survive this.

And if they don't kill him, I will. Even if I have to use my bare hands.

Still, Elijah's misplaced assurance and air of steady determination unnerve me. Something is so very wrong with that man.

Shapes shift in the trees, black shadows materializing from the night. My feet freeze halfway into my next step as my chest tightens and stomach flips around itself.

"Elijah? That you?" calls one man dressed in the familiar League gear, a giant weapon in his hands.

My eyes dart to Ryder, but I can't see his face behind the visor of his helmet, so I sneak a glance at Charlie instead. Whatever thoughts roam her head, they are carefully concealed by her usual calm demeanor. There has to be something on this planet that cracks her poised and solid outer shell. Although, whatever it is, I'm not sure I want to know.

The masked man I know is Nole turns slightly toward Elijah, jerking his head almost imperceptibly. I have a moment of panic believing Elijah won't follow our orders, as he strides forward to stand before his comrade.

"Success," Elijah sneers and a weight lifts off my shoulders. He might be a miserable excuse for a human being, but at least the red-haired psychopath isn't stupid. "I'm taking them to Sawyer."

Elijah's man grins, offering a lazy salute. "Right-O, boss. You called that one good." Then he wanders off, back to whatever post he came from. I figure he'll be one of the first to know Elijah's plan failed when the rest of our party arrives. He'll also be one of the first killed in the coming battle.

In a way, I feel bad for some of the League members. Those who, like myself and Charlie and the rest of the Risers, are only doing what they can to stay alive and joining the League was the best way to ensure survival. Or they were born into it and this seems normal, like all the heinous things I witnessed in ROC that were just part of another day. I bet most of them don't realize how horrible Sawyer and Elijah are, or they've been lead to believe the Risers are the bad guys, just like everyone on the surface believes those in ROC must be as terrible as the Councilmembers. If only the world were that black and white, but like the décor of ROC, it has been painted in a thousand shades of grey. Too many people have been misjudged because of the fanatical ideas of a few.

As the League's mall looms ahead, more than half has been reduced to a giant pile of scorched remains. Only the north side still stands, and I am sad to realize it's the part that houses Sawyer's living quarters and all those creepy, bizarre mannequins he prefers to call "art".

With Ryder and Nole close on his heels, Elijah rounds the back of the building to a small entrance I'd never seen before. Considering the state of the rest of the mall, it's probably one of only two or three useable entrances left, perhaps once intended for employees when the mall was still a mall.

Two guards stand by the doors, but quickly move aside at Elijah's appearance. I have to say, Nole's plan to have Elijah lead us to Sawyer was brilliant. No League member would dare question Elijah, let alone stop him.

Ascending the stairs, guns ready, Elijah leads us through the side of the building and up to the fourth floor. He stops before a small black, metal door and jerks his head at Nole.

"Through there. It's a back hallway to Sawyer's quarters. There won't be any guards until we get to his chambers."

"Well, by all means," Nole says with a jab of his gun. "Shall we?"

"Can you untie me now?" I ask with a hopeful glance at Nole.

"Not yet. Wait till we get through the last guards."

I groan in exasperation, but if I want this mission to be successful, and so far it has, I have no choice but to listen. Besides, it's only a few more minutes, then I can have my hands untied and watch the ropes get transferred straight to Sawyer's wrists. And Elijah's. I hope they'll let me tie the knots. That does seem like ironic justice.

Shouldering through the door, Nole leads us into the hall, Charlie and me next, Ryder and Elijah at our heels and the rest of the League-dressed- Risers trailing along behind. Our boots thud on the tile floor, but there's no reason to be quiet as none of Sawyer's guards will expect anyone other than Elijah and his men with their two captives.

The end of the hall and three armed guards come into sight. One sneers.

"Charlie and that little brat came after all. Gotta say, Elijah, I thought-"

It's the last thing he says as Nole draws a knife from his belt and slashes the man's throat. His gun clatters to the ground as he clutches at the gapping wound in his neck. Blood pours down the front of his uniform, gushing between his fingers as he drops to his knees, choking and convulsing until lying still, all in a matter of seconds.

The two other guards don't even have a chance to react before Risers silence them as well. I turn away from the bodies, breathing heavily, unable to handle death no matter how many times I witness it. I am still struck by how quickly it happens. One moment alive, the next gone, vanished from this earth. Everything involved in that person's life; hopes, dreams, fears, loves, hates; ceasing to exist in a split second, as if none of it ever mattered at all.

I'm sad for the men we've just killed, and for those who will die tonight on both sides, with the exception of Elijah and his grandfather. Some people are too evil to be allowed to exist, and their hopes and dreams or nightmarish delusions need to die too. That is how I cope with the events about to come. Many will die, but at the end of the night, it will be for the best. Some will die so that many others can live.

And isn't that how the Council justifies the Gamble? Does this make me no better than my father, accepting the death of innocent lives just to reach an end goal? I shudder at the thought, but I can't shake away the hints of truth. Jax said that when he stopped caring about the lives of those he kills, then it meant he'd become a monster. Does that mean, in my indifference toward those on the opposing side who will pay the ultimate price tonight, I have become the monster I feared?

Ryder once told me I had a choice, but now it seems that either decision I make, people will be killed. If I refuse to kill Sawyer and Elijah, they will hunt me and anyone I love out of malicious vengeance, but if move forward with this plan, I am condemning dozens to death. Aren't we all here because of me? Destroying the League was my suggestion after all.

So maybe I was always doomed to become a monster. Maybe I never really had a choice, it was only a matter of how and when.

Either way, my time for reflection is long past. Taking a deep breath, I face Ivan and hold out my hands. "Now?"

Laughing to himself and slipping a small knife from his belt, he slices through my ropes and then twists the knife's handle toward me. "Here you go. Hope you're ready."

Grabbing it, I tuck it into my own belt, relieved I'm finally armed.

"Can I have a gun too?" I ask as I see Nole pass one to Charlie. The two share a brief exchange I can't hear, but when Nole reaches out and grazes Charlie's cheek, I can't help but grin. I've decided they make a good couple, and I think Nole is the only man who can match Charlie's intelligence.

The coldness of steel meets my palm, drawing my attention away from our leaders.

"It's had your name on it all night," Ryder says, nodding to the gun I now hold. I find myself once again stepping away from him.

He cocks his head, regarding my odd reaction. "Remember what I told you?"

"Keep the safety on until I'm ready to shoot."

"Good. Now get ready to shoot."

I nod and breathe in again. This is it. This is my last chance. In a few short minutes, either Sawyer will be dead, or I will be. Either way, this ends tonight.

With Elijah in tow, we shove open the door, stride down the short hall and enter Sawyer's chambers.

Where we are met with twenty armed men, all aiming at my tiny group.

Guess I know how it will end. At least I won't have to live with the guilt of becoming a monster.

"Put them down," Elijah snarls, casting a smug smirk at Nole and Charlie. My eyes dart back and forth between them, the rest of my team and the large League army before us. Based on their expressions, somehow I don't think this is part of Nole's plan.

"I said down!" Elijah shouts, features contorted into an even more terrifying version of himself. Immediately, Nole, Charlie and Ryder lower their weapons to the ground. The handful of other Risers follow, with me reluctantly the last to obey.

"And any other weapons," comes the red-haired jerk's next command. Gritting my teeth, I drop my only knife while everyone else tosses aside their own personal arsenals; the repeated clink of metal on linoleum ringing in my ears and killing my hopes one fallen weapon at a time.

Elijah nods at several of the guards who move forward to pat us down and take our weapons. I resist the urge to squirm or slap the man who gropes at my arms and legs.

"Ah!" a voice calls, and I lift my head to see Sawyer's hunched form shuffle into view. "I see we used the back entrance. Guess someone should have warned you that is our fail-safe, a signal that our team has been captured and forced here against their will. Only a select few of my team know about that option, and we've never had a chance to use it before. Glad to know the idea worked, so thank you for that."

I try to gauge Nole and Charlie's reaction, but even though I'm sure this knowledge is new to them, they don't let on.

Waddling forward, as if every joint in his body aches and cracks, Sawyer stops directly in front of me. "Welcome back, Miss Keslin. It's nice to have you in my home once more. We will not be losing you again."

"Bite me, old man," I growl, which only earns me a swift punch to the gut from the League guard beside me. Doubling over, I fall to my knees, gasping for breath and blinded by the pain burning in my lungs.

Sawyer turns to Charlie, arms extended and a half smile on his thin, wrinkled lips. "And Charlotte, my dearest daughter, home again as well."

It takes several seconds for his words to register, but when it does, it expels the air from me once again, as if I were smashed under a giant rock. I feel like I'm going to throw up and black out and have my head explode all at once. Time has slowed down as every eye in the room rests on Sawyer and Charlie. I still can't breathe, but now I'm not sure if it's from the punch to my stomach or the one to my emotions. Sawyer must be lying, some sort of trick to turn us against Charlie or destroy our faith in her or-

"Hi, Dad," she whispers, her gaze never leaving his face. I choke and sputter. It can't be. It's not possible.

And then a new realization hits me and I'm not sure how many more mental blows I can take. If Sawyer is Charlie's father, then that means Elijah, this vile, repulsive man devoid of any empathy whatsoever, and who has murdered in cold-blood, is her son.

Her son.

The words ring through my head like a siren, over and over again. But now I see it. Charlie and Elijah, they have the same eyes. Except where his are filled with madness and hatred, hers are filled with love and hope, making them both look so vastly different, it proved nearly impossible to notice any physical similarities before.

If Nole or Ryder or any of the other Risers already knew, they certainly don't show it on their faces, appearing as stunned and distraught as I am, mouths hanging open. I can only imagine their astonishment as the woman they have either followed or befriended or both, a woman who has fought so strongly against the League, is the daughter and mother of the men who've been bullying them for years. I doubt Charlie ever told anyone the truth, the same way I didn't want to admit who I am when I first arrived on the surface. Justly or otherwise, children are judged by the sins of their parents.

Charlie has started speaking again, but I've been so blinded by incredulity I've missed half of what she's said.

"-is with me. Let the rest of them go. I'll send them away and they won't bother you anymore. Take your revenge on me. That's really where your hatred lies."

"No!" I cry, rising to my knees.

Elijah drives his foot into the back of my ribs and I howl from the new stabbing pain, toppling over and clutching at my side that never fully healed from his last assault.

"Still haven't learned to keep your mouth shut yet, have you Sub?"

A pitiful whimper comes as my only response as I writhe back and forth on the cold, cracked tiles.

"Leave her alone," Charlie commands. Though her voice

never rises above a steady whisper, I still hear the tone of authority.

"You still have a weakness for her kind, don't you?" Sawyer asks with a shake of his head. "You never learned, did you? Why, dear daughter, would you continue to fight for Subs like her? Knowing what they have done?"

"*She* didn't do anything. And I'll fight for her because she is human. Because she escaped the tyranny of her world, just like I did. Because despite your best efforts, I still managed to retain my compassion. I would hardly call any of that weakness."

The old man snorts. "Compassion. And look at where that has gotten you."

"I'd rather die for what is right, than live for what is wrong."

"Oh Charlotte, sweetheart, you won't die. Not today at least. What kind of father would I be if I murdered my only child as she stands defenseless before me? Her son a witness? No. Even I am not that cruel. In fact, I'll let you make a choice."

"A choice?" she asks.

"Yes. Either you kill Kelsey yourself, or I kill all of your friends." He strides toward her, his liver spotted head coming up to her chin. "No matter what, Kelsey dies tonight. You have the choice on whether or not the others walk out of here. How's that for compassion?"

For maybe only the third time since I've met her, Charlie's face betrays her emotions as her expression tumbles into one of evident horror and dread. "Choose? I could never. I won't choose to kill anyone!"

Sawyer shrugs and flips a gnarled hand. "So be it. Then you've chosen to kill them all." With a nod at his guards, several step forward and level guns at Nole and Ryder's heads, and the heads of the men and women with us. Taking a small pistol from one of Sawyer's guards and then kneeling, Elijah jams the barrel of his own weapon against my temple, the cool metal making my blood run cold as my cheek is pressed into the floor.

"I'm going to enjoy this," he jeers, leaning down with his face so close to my own I can feel the warmth of his breath.

I won't close my eyes. If I am going to die today, right now, after all of the other near deaths I have survived, I will not close my eyes and hide from it. I want Elijah to be forced to look into them, to remember them and see them in his dreams. I want to haunt him for the rest of his life. He may well already be one of the monsters Jax fears becoming, but in my final moments, I will pray to whatever gods may be watching that I can find a way to twist into Elijah's mind and infect whatever tiny bit of sanity might still reside in there.

Then the thought of Jax causes tears to sting the back of my eyes because I will never see him again. Or Rey. I said my good-byes though, in the only ways I knew how. I just wish I hadn't left either of them in my self-created limbo, never knowing whom I would choose in the end.

Now the end has arrived, and I still have no idea, longing for one last kiss from either and from both and then hating myself again because they deserve better. Maybe my death will be a good thing, releasing them from the pain and unfairness I have caused. I once promised Daniel I would take care of Jax and instead I've nearly destroyed him.

Someone told me once that right before you die, your life flashes before your eyes. I suppose that might be the case for others, but not for me. The images I see are ones of the people whom my death will save. Jax and Rey will be free to move forward. The Risers, both old and new, will leave, running away from the League to someplace safe, Nadia with them. And without me, Sawyer will never penetrate ROC's defenses so all those innocent people will be safe from whatever massacre the

League has planned. In the end, I'll get everything I wanted.

Maybe my death is a good thing. Like the belief behind the Gamble; the death of one to save the lives of many. This is the gamble we take, right? The fates have finally selected my number.

Elijah cocks his weapon and my entire body tenses, waiting for the gunshot that will end it all, the final sound I'll ever hear. Charlie yells, but over the noise of my heart pounding and my breath coming faster and Elijah chuckling to himself, she sounds miles away.

The quick pop of gunfire comes and in spite of my resolve, I snap my eyes shut. I might want to stare down Elijah, but I don't have the strength to watch my friends die.

And Elijah pulls the trigger.

CHAPTER SIXTEEN

Assuming this is death, I have to say I'm a little disappointed. I expected a pretty white light and a long tunnel and the sensation of floating or flying. Instead, it doesn't feel any different than living did. My cheek remains pressed to a cold, hard surface, my ears ring from the sounds of massive turmoil around me and my ribs still ache every time I...

...Breathe.

I don't like to admit it, but I have no doubt it's true; at some point in this world, my luck will run out. Just apparently not today.

Opening my eyes, Elijah still points the gun at my head, but each time he pulls the trigger, it only clicks, the same way mine did that night in the woods when Ashlynn gave me an unloaded weapon. But why in the world would the League give him an unloaded gun?

Assessing the room around me, bodies litter the floor and someone fires actual loaded guns, the familiar pop of bullets exploding in the giant room as they ricochet off tile floor, marble walls and rusted metal clothing racks.

Nole and Charlie crouch behind a sideways display case, Nole covers her head as his eyes, wide with shock, dart back and forth. Whatever is happening, he didn't anticipate it. Neither did Charlie.

With both Risers and Sawyer's guards in the same uniforms, I have no idea who is shooting at whom, or who I can even call the good guys anymore. All I see are black clad figures in helmets, hoisting automatic weapons over the tops of whatever furniture or around walls people use as cover. Some dash between pillars in search of a better firing position, causing a fresh onslaught of bullets to whiz through the space. Sawyer's bald head is nowhere to be seen.

The squeak of rubber soled shoes on linoleum draws my attention away from the chaos. I turn my head in time to see Elijah running for the back door.

"Oh, hell no," I hiss through clenched teeth as my blood boils. I have no idea what is going on in the room behind me, and while it would probably be safer to hide like Nole and Charlie, I will not allow Elijah to make it through that door.

Surging to my feet, I leap over one of Sawyer's disturbing mannequins, this one painted in bright red berry juice that looks like dried blood. Maybe it is blood, who knows. I soar into the air, arms outstretched as I tackle the orange-haired monster to the ground. We both hit with dull thuds, pain blazing through my right arm as I land on top of Elijah with a grunt.

A fist connects with my jaw, knocking me over onto my back. Spots explode in my vision and I shake them away, but before I can regain full consciousness and stand straight, Elijah smacks me again, sending me flat against the floor as a sharp pain spreads across my face

He runs for the door a second time. I stagger to my feet, head swimming as I reach out for the wall to steady myself, tripping over that stupid mannequin in the process.

Its left arm has been kicked loose. Snatching it up, I beam it at Elijah, the hollow plastic limb colliding with the back of his head, causing him to stumble to one knee with a yelp. At least the mannequin was useful for something. That's artwork I can enjoy.

Pouncing again, I drive my elbow into the center of his back, right between his shoulder blades. He arches back and howls in a mixture of agony and anger before flipping around and striking out with one leg. I fling my body sideways and find myself face to face with a knife lying on the floor, lost from someone else's belt in the chaos.

Elijah slides across the floor as I jerk the weapon into my hands. I slash out, aiming for his neck but slicing his shoulder with a six-inch gash instead. A red ribbon of blood flows from the wound, soaking the sleeve of his shirt and dripping down his arm. Rearing backward, clutching at the wound, eyes glittering with his psychotic wrath, Elijah laughs at me. "You'll never win."

Shoving to my feet, I prepare to attack a third time, but he picks up what remains of the mannequin's body and hurls it my direction. I try to duck, but move too slow and the torso smacks into my chest, flinging me back to the floor yet again. My head smacks the base of the wall behind me, denting the drywall. I groan as my vision fades in and out.

As I struggle to regain control of my senses, Elijah's form disappears through the back door. By the time I recover and slam through it into the stairwell, he's gone.

In fury I chuck the knife down the staircase, its metal blade ringing off the handrails and rattling against concrete walls before it comes to rest on the landing two flights down.

"Hey now, ya just got the thing," a voice says. I spin to face Ryder, his face drenched with perspiration and speckles of blood. A gash runs the length of his forehead, streaming blood into one eye and down his cheek before dripping off his chin. It must look worse than it is though, since he's standing. A gun hangs in his right hand and he favors his left leg slightly.

"Elijah got away!" I shout, unable to control my rage and frustration. Balling a fist, I slam it against the metal railing with a dull thud. Pain flows through my wrist and up my arm, but I barely notice. Instead, I turn and pound it into the stairwell wall, driving a hole through it and bruising my knuckles.

I was so close to this being over. To never having to worry about Elijah prowling around the next corner or living in fear that no matter where I hide, he will still find me.

Sobs break loose, choking and painful and I bury my face into my palms. "He got away."

"Come on now," Ryder says, tucking me under one of his thick, muscular arms. Reminded of the night he shot the League man without so much as a second thought or a bit of remorse, I jerk away in repulsion.

Ryder scowls, wrinkles creasing deeper on his bloodied forehead. "What's up, kid? You've been avoidin' me."

"No, I haven't."

"I'm not stupid. Least not as stupid as I look. You've been keepin' your distance since the night we had security duty, which I know you lied to me 'bout to get away from Jax or whatever was goin' on with your boyfriends."

"They aren't my boyfriends."

"Like I said, whatever. I don't care about the love lives of a bunch of eighteen-year-olds. I do care about why you suddenly seem sickened by me."

I say nothing, jaw tense and grinding as I stand in the stairwell with my arms crossed tight over my chest.

"Fine. Let's see if I can guess. This got anything to do with that guy I shot?"

"You didn't have to shoot him!" I burst, all my anger at Elijah and Sawyer and the failed mission boiling over.

"Have to shoot him? Debatable. Couldn't run real fast or far with a bullet hole in his shoulder. Wanted to shoot him? Heck yes. He'd have done the same to either of us and I got some good satisfaction outta it."

I'm still crying, though I have no idea over what this time. I could be crying over one of so very many things I've lost count. My teeth grind together as I glare at Ryder.

"Listen kid, I am not a hero. Never have been, never will be and sure don't wanna be. Don't get me wrong though, I'm not the villain either. But don't try to paint me black or white. This world is filled with ten thousand colors and not a single person on it will fit as black or white or even grey. I don't give a crap about most of the other people on this planet. I know what I am. You've had a hard road and I'm sure it's gonna get harder, but your journey has yet to compare to mine. When you've been tested the way I have, seen the things I've seen and been forced to do some of the things I've done, you come back and let me know what colors you are. I'll bet you don't even have a palette big enough to figure it out."

I avert my eyes, staring at the cement floor, thinking about how it looks so much like ROC. Then my thoughts turn to what I did just to escape ROC, how I was willing to give up my whole life, even willing to kill another person. And I think of all the things I've been faced with since coming to the surface. The things I've done.

"We choose who we become," I whisper.

"Yes, we do. I've chosen to be a survivor, plain and simple. Now, we may have lost that piece of scum, Elijah, but we did get that disgustin' old man."

I lift my gaze, daring to hope. "Sawyer?"

"Come see."

"Did... did you know who he was? Do you know about Charlie?"

Ryder licks his chapped lips and wipes at the blood on his face, only managing to smear it more. "No. I don't think anyone knew. I've always known Charlie carried her own secrets, but this... I didn't expect this. But I also don't expect it to change anythin'. Charlie is still the same person we've chosen to follow and the same person we care about. Now, come on and let's figure out what just happened, cause I got a few questions."

We re-enter the mall, the smells of blood and gunpowder and sweat overwhelming. League guards and Risers stand in a small clump. Everyone appears slightly uneasy, but all aim their weapons to the floor. Nole and Charlie stand in the center talking with one man with greying dark hair and a long, narrow face and ears that jut out almost sideways. A week's worth of stubble lines his chin and a thin hooked nose seems to almost reach to his top lip.

Ryder and I approach with caution, nudging through the throngs of both friends and enemies. I glance between the others.

"So, why..." I begin, but stop when I realize I don't even know what questions to ask.

"Kelsey," Charlie says, directing my attention to the man, "this is Sawyer's second in command, Neil Thomas."

I blink a few times and give him a good up and down before looking back at Charlie. "And we're all standing around talking like old friends because...?"

"Because we are old friends," she says, though her face shows no joy, only a broken, painful sorrow and sheer exhaustion. "Neil and I grew up together. I had no idea he'd been placed in this position."

Whatever meaning all this has is lost on me as I stand dumbstruck in the middle of the circle of people who should be firing bullets at each other.

The man, Neil, clears his throat and rubs his face. "We've been planning an uprising against Sawyer and Elijah for the last several months. Their tyrannical mission and sick lack of any empathy has done nothing but destroy countless lives. We had no idea Nole and Charlie planned an attack tonight, but when my men and I were summoned to Sawyer's chambers for protection against a blind infiltration, we knew it was now or never."

"So instead of shooting us, you shot Sawyer's guards? Whichever ones weren't on your side?" I ask for clarification.

"Yes."

"And gave an empty gun to Elijah?"

"That too."

I turn to Nole and Charlie. "You guys really had no plan to get out of Sawyer's trap?"

They share a look and then both shake their heads.

"No," Nole replies. "I had no idea of any of this. I thought we were... I thought we'd lost. You can imagine my surprise when Neil and his men started attacking the other League members instead of us. Though not nearly as surprised as Sawyer I'd imagine."

"Where is Sawyer?" I demand, unable to fathom just how lucky we all are. Sure, Elijah escaped, but technically, we should all be dead now anyway, so maybe I can deal with Elijah still loose in the world. Can't be picky with my life on the line.

The crowd parts, Neil stepping aside to reveal a crumpled figured on the ground lying in a widening pool of crimson blood.

I force myself to swallow, my throat tightening as my stomach performs a complicated variation of twists and flips. Shuffling forward, I shift closer and closer to the body until Sawyer's face comes into view. A small round bullet hole pierces his forehead, shattering out the back of his skull. Just like his grandson had done to Ashlynn. Empty, lifeless hazel eyes stare unblinking into nothingness. Like those ROC citizens whose murders he ordered.

The room tilts and my knees go out from under me, but Ryder snatches me with one arm, placing me back on my feet as understanding dawns.

We've survived. I've survived. Sawyer is finally dead. The League is no more.

"Who?" I manage to choke out. "Who did it?"

"I did," Charlie says, her voice wavering and as I whip around to face her, I see she is on the verge of tears and fighting so valiantly to not cry in front of me or Ryder or everyone else that looks to her for leadership and guidance.

She killed Sawyer. Charlie killed her father. Her father who was insane and she has a son who is a monster. And yet she still cares, that much is written so plainly on her face it's as though someone tattooed it there like my barcode; the grief, the burning agony, the knowledge that she had no other choice. It was kill or be killed.

Knowing she might not like it, but also knowing I don't care, I rush forward and hug her. At first, she stands strong and tall, returning the embrace stiffly, but after a moment her weight falls into my arms and she begins to cry, her tears dampening the shoulder of my shirt.

Then Nole's beside us, pulling her away and into his own arms.

"Charlie," he whispers, brushing auburn hair from her face. "I'm so sorry."

He leads her away into a dark corner of the ancient store, behind more of those disconcerting mannequins. I want to set fire to every single one. We can make a party of it.

"Kelsey!" I hear someone shout, turning in time to see Rey push through the crowd that has formed around Sawyer's dead body.

Rey's face is strained, eyes wild and blond curls tangled

and matted with sweat. As he moves closer, I see blood splatters his skin and his shirt and even the waistband of his pants.

"Rey!" I cry in a mixture of shock and alarm, having not expected to see him... well, ever again actually. "Rey, what happened? Are you hurt?"

Kelsey!" he calls again, spotting me in the throng of people who have turned their attention from the dead man to stare at Rey instead. He stops only a few feet away, motioning for me to follow him back to the main section of the mall, or whatever remains in the aftermath of the fire from a few days ago. His face turns somber. "Follow me. It's... it's Jax. He's been shot."

It's as if someone has smashed me across the face with a rock. I falter backward, the air whooshing from my lungs.

Someone latches onto my arm, pulling me out of the tunnel surrounding my vision. It's Rey. He's talking so fast through his labored breathing I almost miss what he says.

"Jax saved me, jumped in front of a bullet meant for my head. You need to come. He keeps asking for you."

Relief floods through me. "He's awake?"

"He was. I don't know now." Rey stops suddenly, clasping my shoulder and biting his lips. "Kels... it's bad."

I can only nod and swallow, my tongue and throat so dry no words will slide past. My mind wants to wander to the worst possible scenario; that once again I am going to watch someone die. Someone who will die because I couldn't follow the rules. Someone I love.

Shoving the horrifying thoughts away, refusing to allow them to take over my emotions, I stumble through the marble halls after Rey. Blood soaks every surface and bodies litter the floor. League members, compound members, Risers. I search each face, praying I recognize none.

One looks at me with opened, lifeless eyes and I am reminded again, of all people, of Ashlynn and how her emerald green eyes looked so doll-like in death. I stop staring at the faces and keep my eyeline trained on the back of Rey's head. I set up invisible, mental blinders between the carnage and myself. If I am going to survive whatever I find next, I need my mind as clear as possible.

We round a small corner leading to one set of the mall's exterior doors. A small group of people huddles in a tight circle. The mood hangs tense and ominous.

Willing myself forward, forcing my feet to comply, I push through the outer edge of the group until I stand over a woman who kneels beside Jax. She presses someone's shirt to his chest, though now it's so saturated with blood I have no idea what color it once had been.

Jax lies prone on the cold, hard floor, one leg twisted oddly beneath him and arms splayed out to the sides. Fresh blood coats both his shirt and the broken brown tiles underneath him. His eyes are open, though I don't think he really sees anything as they drift around, a glassy haze enveloping his vision.

"Kelsey," he mumbles. "Where's Kelsey?"

I choke back a sob, falling to my knees next to him and taking one hand in my own. His skin feels cold to the touch, a greyish tinge setting in. He gasps and whimpers, his breath so weak I wait for each one to be his last. With a shudder, Jax's teeth clack together.

I can feel death beside me, gazing over my shoulder as he waits to claim Jax for his own. I am powerless to stop him.

"I'm right here Jax," I whisper, brushing sweat-drenched hair from his face. Cold perspiration has broken out along his brow and upper lip, somehow making him look even more pale and ghostly. Even his eyes seem drained of their brilliant hues.

"Is Kelsey safe?" he asks, eyes wandering around, flicking over my face but registering nothing. This time I can't control the sobs erupting from my chest. I flip my head to all the people just standing around watching Jax die.

"Is anyone going to do something?" I demand, hearing the shrill note of rising insanity in my tone. Everyone looks at the person next to them or at the floor or the ceiling, anywhere except me. Their expressions look hopeless, no one wanting to voice the truth.

I fist my hands in my hair, pulling at the curls. "There has to be something we can do! We can't just let him die!"

"Kelsey," someone says and Lara pushes forward to squat beside me, sadness written across her sharp, angular features. "The bullet went through the upper right side of his chest and out the back. It definitely cracked his collar bone, though we think it missed his lung. But every time he breathes, he loses more blood and we have no way to stop it. Not here at least. Without the right supplies, and our doctor, Camrie to help him, there's nothing we can do."

My gaze returns to Jax, he's muttering, but too softly for me to make out what as his head tosses from side-to-side. He has minutes left at most and a wrenching pain tugs at my heart, as if someone intends to rip it from my body.

I wring his limp hand, smooth his damp hair and whisper into his ear, praying he'll understand. "I wasn't lying earlier, Jax. I really do love you. I'm so sorry it's ending like this."

Even though Rey stands less than two feet away, I won't repeat a mistake I've already regretted once. Leaning down, I kiss Jax softly, one last time.

CHAPTER SEVENTEEN

As I break away, I see Jax's eyes are closed, breathing labored as he has slipped into a final oblivion. I wish I could stare at his eyes, commit their beautiful turquoise to memory, but maybe it's better this way, he won't feel any more pain. If only there was a way to stop the blood pumping from the small round hole in his chest. It's almost amazing how one tiny little object can destroy so much, kill one life and shatter so many others in a matter of seconds. If we were in ROC, they'd be able to save him. They have real doctors and stitches and-

And...

An idea collides into my mind, scattering my emotions and giving me one flutter of hope to cling to. I remember watching Rey do it once when he cut his arm at work. The deep wound wouldn't stop bleeding, but Rey couldn't afford stitches or medical attention, so he took care of the problem on his own, me beside him for moral support. It sickened me then and it's absolutely nuts now, but what do I have to lose at this point? What does Jax have to lose? If I don't, he's dead in two minutes.

A lantern sits on the other side of Jax, the flame still flickering, ignorant to the devastation. Grabbing the handle, I surge to my feet and rush to an old wooden bench resting in a mangled heap in a corner.

"What are you do-" Rey calls, but I ignore him as I raise the lantern over my head and hurl it with all my strength at the pile of dry, rotting wood. The lantern shatters, fuel racing free and immediately igniting on the ancient piece of dry, broken furniture as the lantern flame transforms into a blazing fire.

Sliding Ryder's knife from my belt, I jab it into the flames, my skin burning and blistering in the heat. Welts form and pop on my fingers, but I grit my teeth, and force myself not to pull away until I know the blade has grown hot enough.

"Cut open his shirt!" I order, hurrying back to Jax's supine form. No one moves. "NOW!"

Rey drops to the floor, grabbing the neckline of Jax's T-shirt and ripping it down the middle, exposing Jax's bare, blood-soaked chest.

I kneel again, holding the hot knife in my throbbing hand. "I'm really sorry Jax, this is gonna hurt." Not sure why I bothered to say anything. It's not like he can hear me.

Pressing the steel blade to the wound on his chest, his skin sizzles and smokes. The smell of cooking flesh waifs into my nostrils, causing me to gag and swallow the rising bile, turning my head as far from the stench as possible.

Whatever unconsciousness Jax had slipped into wasn't enough. His eyes pop open, wide with fright as a scream of agony bursts from his lips.

"Flip him over," I order. Rey rolls Jax until he lies on his side, whimpering in his pain-induced semi-consciousness. Together, Rey and I remove the tattered remains of his shirt and with a deep breath, I press the knife to the jagged, bloody exit wound.

Jax cries again and again as the wound is cauterized shut, until finally the blood no longer flows and his screams go silent and I know he's thankfully blacked out.

Rey slumps down beside me as I sit back on my heels, panting from the ordeal. Burned welts have erupted on Jax's skin, red and slimy and in some places charred black, but he's alive. At least for now. Hopefully for always if I have any say in the matter. I drop the knife, clutching my burned hand to my chest as the searing pain sets in.

"Where did you learn to do that?" Lara asks, her jaw slack with shock. The others stare at me too, their expressions an odd combination of revulsion and admiration.

"I did it once," Rey replies, pulling back the sleeve of his shirt to display the old burn scar. "Kelsey watched me do it."

"Bleeding stopped," is all I say as I stare at the crimson puddle around Jax. I can't believe it's all his. I can't believe it's all his and he's somehow still alive.

Nodding slowly, Lara crouches beside Jax, checking his pulse and breath. "He's weak, still lost a lot of blood and will be at risk for infection, but if the bullet missed his lung and he makes it through the next couple days, he might be ok. You saved his life."

Everything feels surreal. The entire night feels like some twisted, macabre combination of a horrific nightmare and a wonderful dream.

I lift my head to the group of Risers around me, because whether we came from Charlie's compound or not, we are all Risers now. Taking each face in turn, I manage a small smile. "Sawyer is dead."

Their eyes widen, lips parting in round 'O's' of surprise as they dart glances back and forth between each other.

"Really?" Lara asks, her voice so filled with hope. I remember that she hid in Sawyer's ranks for over a year, watched his callous insanity firsthand and also watched her friend die because of him. She probably wanted Sawyer dead as much as anyone.

"Yes. I saw it with my own eyes. Elijah though, he escaped."

A stocky, middle-aged man behind Lara snorts. "Whatever. Sawyer's dead, as well as half his little militia. Most of the others have scattered in fear. Elijah has no one behind him, no support and no one to help. He might as well be dead for all the good an escape did him. We won the war."

The man brings up valid points, but I'd still be considerably more at ease if I saw Elijah's corpse myself and had a chance to nudge it around with my foot. Maybe burn the body just to be sure. And then throw a celebration over his death.

Then a wave of guilt crashes over me because this is Charlie's son and as horrific a person as he is, I'm sure a part of Charlie still loves him and would forever grieve his death.

"So now what?" Rey asks. "Even with the League destroyed, I don't really want to stay in their headquarters, but I doubt Jax will survive a trip all the way back to the Risers' building."

"Charlie's safe house," I blurt. "The one we used the first time I was rescued from the League. It's just a few miles. If we can find a way to transport him, we can stay there until he's well enough to go home. There must be others injured as well who can't travel all the way back home."

Everyone nods and murmurs in agreement. Two men leave to find wood or something to use as a make-shift gurney. I return my attention to Jax, wrapping my fingers between his again and brushing my injured hand through his hair, sticky with drying blood and perspiration and dirt. I wish I had water and a cloth to clean his face and wounds but that will have to wait.

Someone clasps my shoulder and I look up to see Rey hovering over me. I'd nearly forgotten he was here and I consider dropping Jax's hand for a moment, hoping I don't hurt Rey's feelings, but the look on my best friend's face indicates he understands. Right now, this isn't about who loves who more or less or what. It's about Jax, who nearly died saving Rey's life, needing support and comfort so he can recover.

"I'm gonna find Charlie and Nole," Rey says. "Update them on everything out here and see if they need any help rounding up the last of Sawyer's soldiers. Do you need anything?"

I shake my head. "Thank you, Rey. For everything you've done for me." I squeeze his hand, momentarily connecting all three of us.

A smile slides over Rey's lips as he nods and let's go. I can't help but think his smile, once so full of life and mischief and everything that made him Rey, now looks sad and empty. I don't have time to dwell on it though because he flips around, his long, lanky gait carrying him back toward Sawyer's chambers.

* * *

In less than an hour, we've lashed Jax to the seat of an old metal bench and several men now carry him from the League's mall, Lara and I in tow. Others follow, carrying more of the wounded while Nole and Charlie stay behind to assess the dead.

Slipping into the woods, I give the mall one last look of smug defiance. We won. If I have any say in the matter, this will be the last time I ever set foot in that building. I wish we had time and resources to burn the rest of the thing down just like Elijah burned Charlie's compound.

We all travel in silence, me pacing alongside Jax's makeshift gurney so I can hold his hand. He hasn't woken and his complexion is so pale and ashen, I repeatedly check for a pulse, heaving an exhale of relief every time I find it, however weak it might be.

By the time we finally reach the safe house, dawn hovers on the horizon, a hazy mist of humidity hanging in front of the ruby red sun. I love the warmth. Inside ROC, the public areas and halls weren't climate controlled to conserve resources, and the rationing of oil left most of the private suites, or at least those who could afford it, at a cool sixty-six degrees. It never occurred to me that the air could be warm, like a heated blanket wrapped around my bare skin.

Following the men carrying Jax upstairs, they place him in one of the many old bedrooms onto a squeaking, rickety bed with tattered, dust covered blankets. Lara fetches a bucket of water from the well, returning to the room just as I've managed to slice off the last bits of Jax's shredded shirt.

"Thanks," I say, taking the bucket and a clean cloth.

"You should get some sleep," she says with a pat on my shoulder. "You've had a long night. I can clean him up."

I shake my head. "It's ok. I want to be here if he wakes up and I doubt I'll be able to sleep all that much anyway."

"Ok, but don't forget to take care of yourself too," she says, indicating my burned hand. Then she squeezes through the bedroom door, shutting it behind her with a muffled click.

Ringing out the rag in the bucket, I wipe the sweat and filth from his face first. Some color has returned to his cheeks, though not enough for me to think he's out of the woods. There's still the strong possibility of infection from either the burns or the original wound. Without access to medication, an infection will almost certainly kill him. But for right now he doesn't run a fever and he breathes normally. Lara seems to think the bullet missed his lung by a matter of a few inches. I'm still waiting for Camrie to come give her medical assessment. She has so many people to attend to tonight.

Gently scrubbing the dried blood from his chest, I'm careful not to press too hard on his burned skin, not wanting to cause him anymore pain. Once I've cleaned him as best I can, I clean my hand and wrap it in fresh cloth. Then I set the bucket aside, draw my chair closer to his bed and lay my head down until it rests beside his shoulder. I interlace our fingers, watch his chest rise and fall and offer up a silent plea to whomever listens that they please let Jax live.

After all, I promised Daniel I'd always take care of Jax. He has to live, or else I've broken my promise.

He stirs slightly, a soft moan escaping on his weak breath. I lift my head. "Jax?"

His eyes flutter open, their bright green- blue standing in drastic contrast to his black hair and pale skin. It reminds me of a photograph I saw once years ago where everything had been color corrected to black and white; except the subject's eyes, which were a piercing shade of deep green with a hazel ring and tiny gold flecks. Being the only color in the photo, the girls' eyes became the focal point, giving her an air of mysterious authority and radiant beauty. I often wondered who the girl had been, what happened to the photo, why I don't even remember where I saw it but can still remember every detail of her eyes.

"Hey, Kelsey," Jax murmurs with the smallest hint of a smile, probably the most he can manage right now.

I grin, running a finger along his cheek. "Hey. How do you feel?"

"Like a giant bucket of garbage. My shoulder is burning."

"I know. I burned you."

He blinks a few times in confusion. "What? I thought I got shot?"

"You did. I burned the wound closed or you would have lost too much blood. Jax, you nearly died."

I didn't intend to cry. I swore to myself I'd hold the tears at bay because I have no right to cry. He was there, once again, because of me. He got shot saving my best friend who he doesn't even like. While I know I can't blame myself for what happened, I have no right to cry in front of Jax when he's risked so much for me and I've risked almost nothing for him in return. I feel selfish and self-centered and terrified that someone I love will die because I haven't chosen to be better.

But despite my attempts, the tears fall anyway, dainty rivers dribbling down to my chin before splashing onto the wrinkled, faded bed sheets.

Lifting his head a few inches, Jax runs a thumb across my damp skin. "Why are you crying? I'm fine. I'm mostly fine. I've told you a million times that-"

"I know, I know," I interrupt with a strangled laugh. "It's gonna take a lot more than the stupid League to take you out of this world."

"Glad we're finally on the same page," he says, letting his head flop back to the pillow. "It does hurt like crap though. Guess this time the League came pretty close to making a liar out of me. What's the verdict? Do I get to keep the arm? I mean, I've had it for longer than I can remember."

His voice holds a tone of amusement, but I can hear the genuine concern masked beneath. I want to be reassuring and tell him everything will be alright, but he'll know I'm lying.

"It's too soon to tell," I reply. "The bullet went straight through and missed your lung, or at least that's what Lara said, but there's still a risk of infection and we have no idea what other damage it may have done. The fact you're awake right now is a good sign though."

"Yeah well, I kinda wish I wasn't."

"I'm sorry, Jax. I know you're in a lot of pain."

"I guess you would know. You realize that you got shot before me? The ROC kid who never even touched a real gun until her eighteenth birthday gets shot before the rugged, tough surface-boy who has been handling guns and staring down the barrels of them for most of his life. To be honest, I felt like I was missing out before."

He traces the barcode on my wrist with his thumb. "Now

we both have barcodes and bullet holes. The mark of your world and the mark of mine."

The words sting. The reminder that I'm still not really part of Jax's world, that I still carry the mark of ROC forever inked on my skin. I know he didn't mean to upset me, if anything, I have no doubt that Jax now views us as equals, but I pull away from his touch anyway. "Do you need anything? Water? Some food?"

With his good arm, he reaches out for me, bring me back toward him. "Can you stay here with me? Is that ok?"

I smile. "Of course I can."

Sliding the chair closer, I turn it sideways so I can partially stretch out with my head next to his, half my body on his bed and the other half on the chair. I'm reminded of way he slept when I once laid in bed injured thanks to the League. Somehow, Jax and I always end up being equal, the same, as if we were carved from the same material. Tattoos and demons. It's strange how two people from such very different backgrounds, can become so similar after all.

He pulls my hand up until it rests on the center of his chest, his skin warm and damp with perspiration from the start of a fever. Within a few moments his breathing begins to slow.

"Thank you," he whispers, groggy with the first vestiges of sleep. "For saving me."

"Thank you for saving Rey."

"I had to. For you. If he died, I knew you'd die too."

I wish I could say that isn't true, but I know I'd be lying. Isn't that how we all ended up here in the first place? After everything I've been through, after meeting and falling in love with Jax, having Rey return from the dead, I remember what happened when I thought I'd lost him once before. I can't stand the idea of it ever happening again.

But I also can't say it would be any different if Jax died. Pieces of my soul have become so intertwined with both of them, as if they are part of the lifeblood keeping me alive. Should anything happen to either of them, I will never survive.

CHAPTER EIGHTEEN

I wake late the following night, well after dinnertime, shocked that I slept for probably close to eighteen hours. Stretching my stiff neck, causing the bones to pop, and shaking my right arm that tingles from having fallen asleep, I take a moment to check on Jax. His condition seems unchanged from the night before though there's no denying the heat of the fever on his brow. He still snores, lying flat on his back with his mouth hanging open.

My stomach gives a dissatisfied grumble, which is understandable considering I haven't eaten in over a day. Giving Jax one last glance, I tiptoe from the room to find food. I know some of the others brought packs with them just in case we couldn't return to the compound right away. Ryder always has fat, juicy apples because I'm pretty sure that's all he eats. And large chunks of rare meat.

Then I realize I haven't seen him since Rey found me last night. Nor have I seen Charlie. I wonder if they're here or if they went all the way back to the compound. They might not even know about Jax, having so many other injured or dead to handle.

Finding my way to the first floor, I poke my head into several empty rooms in search of either the food packs, or someone in charge to update me on the rest of last night's happenings. As I turn down a narrow, wood paneled hallway, muffled voices drift from behind a closed door at the opposite end. Moving closer I recognize Nole's baritone voice.

"We'd need more manpower. Even without losing men in the battles with the League, and more like Raoul and Nathan who've set off to form their own group elsewhere, we still don't have nearly enough. Ten to one at best."

"There are people inside willing to fight too," someone replies. "I'm not sure how many exactly, they'd never say, but at least a hundred. Maybe more."

"Rey?" I whisper to myself in surprise. What could he and Nole possibly be discussing? Silent as one of the rabbits in the forest, I position myself inches from the closed door. If Elsa were here, she'd punish me for eavesdropping, especially on a leader which is illegal in ROC, but she isn't here and this isn't ROC. Didn't Jax tell me once that rules are a little different on the surface? Why not use that to my advantage?

"Well, that works in our favor I suppose," Nole says. "But without any way to contact them and confirm numbers, we can't use that as part of the plan until we get there, provided your point of contact hasn't been discovered yet."

"Maybe we can appeal to that group to the west," I hear Charlie respond. "I have a decent connection with Asandra. I think we can convince her to join our cause, or at least give her people the option. They have about as much to lose or gain as we do."

"That would be far more beneficial," Nole says. "Of course, that brings us to the next question of how do we get in?"

"Same way I got out," Rey replies. "We have a team that can climb down the airshaft I escaped through. It'll take us into the chambers located in Sector C and we can infiltrate from there. A group could head for the armory, one for the tech station and another to open the exterior door from the inside. If we go at night, follow my instructions and get in contact with Jericho once inside, by the time the Gendarme see us on the camera monitors and get themselves mobilized, we can be spread out through all five sectors. They'll never expect an attack from the surface."

My breath catches, my throat clenching so tightly I almost choke on my own saliva. They're talking about ROC. They want to break in ROC.

Without thinking, I fling open the door and storm into the room, much to the surprise of Nole, Charlie and Rey.

"Are you people insane?" I demand as they all appear too stunned at my entrance to say anything.

"Kelsey!" Charlie exclaims, her features wide in shock.

"Told you so," Rey says matter-of-factly to Nole with a hand flourish my direction. "You all didn't need to worry about me saying anything. She figured it out all on her own."

Scratching his head before smoothing his thick black hair back into place, Nole rises from his chair and moves around me to shut, and this time lock, the door to the hall. He then turns to me, mouth drawn into a tight line of annoyance. "You should sit."

"You're going to attack ROC, aren't you?"

"Miss Keslin, it really would be best if you took a seat right now."

"Do you all realize what will happen to you? They will kill you! All of you! You don't even understand what you're up against down there. The Gendarme are better armed than the League, you have cameras everywhere, and entire team of-"

"Kels," Rey says, "can you seriously just sit down for sec?" He motions to the chair Nole has vacated. Pursing my lips, I glance between the three other occupants, all of whom look exhausted and I wonder if they even slept today, or just immediately began to plan the next war.

"Kelsey," Rey says again, pointing at the chair. "If you'll just hear us out."

Plopping into the seat, I cross my arms over my chest and

offer Nole a look of challenge. I'm not sure what reasoning he can give that will ever make me think this is a good idea.

"In response to your question," Nole says, "though I realize it was rhetorical, yes, we are planning to infiltrate ROC."

"But why? Charlie said they've left you all alone for like, almost fifteen years."

"They have, but that doesn't mean they haven't attacked or even eradicated other surface groups in that time and we'd never know. Nor does it mean they aren't planning something larger against all of us. Their mission is to wipe out all rebels on the surface, including us. It's why ROC was founded in the first place. If they ever want to return to the surface, they must first complete their mission."

I shake my head in fervent disagreement. "No. My father would never..."

Never what? Never kill people? Thanks to his lies and the continuation of the Gamble, he already has, my mother included. What makes me think that he would sentence the one he was supposed to love to death, but opt against killing total strangers who threaten the entire underground world he controls so carefully? I had made a promise to myself that I would no longer bury my head in the dirt and pretend my father and the rest of the Council members aren't some kind of monsters all their own. I've spent my whole life buried, now it's time to see the light, see my father for who he really is.

Lost, I stare vacantly around at my best friend and the two people who have risked so much to keep me alive. They've done more for me than anyone in ROC has even considered. These people have become my family now.

"Can we have a few minutes?" Rey asks, addressing Nole and Charlie. Sharing a quick glance, they both nod and quietly slip from the room, leaving Rey and I alone.

For a tense minute, neither of us speaks, choosing instead to hold the other's gaze, waiting for the other to back down first. We've done this ever since we were little. Normally it's Rey who agrees to come around to my side. I used to think it was because I was always right, now I wonder if it isn't because he's always been in love with me and just wanted me to be happy.

Whatever his reasoning in the past, he does not seem to have any intention of backing down this time.

"Rey," I whisper. "You can't be serious about this?"

"Why not?" he asks in challenge, his voice steady but his eyes full of an anger so alien to him, I almost wonder if he's been possessed.

"Because it will get all of us killed."

"You don't know that. Besides, if we do nothing, we're dead anyway. It's only a matter of time before they come after us, come after the compounds here on the surface. It's like sitting inside ROC waiting for the next Gamble, wondering if our number will be drawn and knowing the odds are worse the longer we stay alive. I refuse to live like that anymore. I'd rather take action now than wait for ROC to do it."

"Fine, but right now we have an advantage we never realized we had in ROC. We could leave. All of us. You and I could convince Charlie and Nole to take the Risers and get as far from ROC as possible."

"And do what? Hide?" he demands, his angelic face darkened into a harsh scowl.

"And forget."

Moving so quickly, I don't have a chance to react, Rey storms forward. He yanks my burned right arm, twisting it around until my wrist stops less than two inches from my nose, the black tattooed barcode and numbers all I can see. The small scar from where Jax cut out my tracker. I cry out and try to pull away, but his grip is too strong, fingers pressed against the bones in my wrist so tightly I worry if he might actually break something.

"Tell me you didn't forget!" he shouts, shaking my arm in my face. "Tell me you didn't forget what they've done to us! To everyone in the O.Z, all those lives that have been lost from the rations and illness and the damn Gamble! My cousins are down there. My friends. Your friends, Elsa, people we care about and people who don't deserve anything that has happened to them. People who could have a chance at life if it weren't for the Council controlling their entire world! How are we supposed to just forget about them?"

Just as suddenly has he grabbed it, Rey releases my arm, letting it fall back to my side as his face transforms into an expression of despair and regret that is enough to splinter my already cracking heart. "Please, Kels, tell me you didn't forget."

Turning away, shoulders crumpling forward, he walks to a nearby window and places one hand on the dusty glass. For the first time since I saw him that night in the woods, I realize how old he looks. He's no longer the impish, vibrant eighteen-year old boy I grew up with. Now he's become a lost, broken shell of himself; void of all of the things that I had grown to love; someone who has lived an entire lifetime of trials and tribulations that have left him less of who he once was. I am gazing upon the shattered remnants of a life of tragedy.

An intense, debilitating sadness washes over me, rubbing my insides raw. I want my best friend back, the Rey that laughed with me and pulled childish pranks during lessons and somehow always found a way to make me smile. The Rey who tampered with cameras just to spend five minutes with me and risked his number in the Gamble so I could have a sugar cookie on my birthday. I don't know who this new Rey is, this grown man filled with rage and hatred, looking for revenge.

I want to hug him. I want to tell him that it's ok to be

broken. I'm a little broken too. Maybe, together, we can each become a full person again and learn to fix ourselves. I want to touch him and kiss him and find my lifelong friend again. I want to bring back the boy I love who may very well have died in those gas chambers after all.

But instead I stand, my feet rooted to the floor because I don't know what to do with Rey. I don't know if there is anything I can do anymore to save him.

"Rey," I finally murmur. "I didn't forget. I'll never forget, but we're up here, alive and together. That's all I could possibly ask for. Going back to ROC, what purpose would that serve other than to lose more lives?"

"Do you know that today is May fifteenth?" he asks, his back still to me as one finger traces along the frame of the window, paint chips being brushed to the floor. "There's a family on the second floor of the Risers' compound and the wife keeps a calendar for everyone, creates a new one each year. Today is May fifteenth, which means the last Gamble was exactly one month ago. One month ago when my number was selected."

Turning back to me, his face a mask of sorrow that strains at my heart, he leans against the window, the old wood of the frame creaking slightly. "The Gamble has taken everything from me; my dad first, then my mom, and eventually any hope I had of a better life for myself where I wouldn't have to increase my odds of death just to have the chance to live."

"And then I was finally getting the one thing in this world I truly wanted. You. Until the Gamble took that too, separated us and now, even though you're here with me again, it's not the same. I can still feel that separation between us, Kels, like whatever bond we once had has been sliced apart with a knife. But instead of healing, the wound has festered and decayed, growing wider and wider and I've begun to realize we'll never be the same again."

He hangs his head, unable to meet my eyes and I think it's because he's trying not to cry. In all the years I've known him, there were only two times ever when he cried. Once when his mother left for the chambers, and again when his aunt got sick and died and he entered his number extra times to afford food for his cousins.

Eventually he regains composure and lifts his head. Tears don't line his face, but his eyes are so deeply, depressingly sad I think that tears would be better.

"No matter how much I love you, Kelsey, the moment my number was called, it sealed our fate and took you from me for forever. Sometimes... sometimes I wish I had never escaped. Sometimes I wish I had stayed in that chamber and died with everyone else. Death would have been easier than this."

Against my better judgment because I don't know how this new, tortured Rey will react, I rush forward and embrace him. My arms wrap so tight around his thin body, I'm not sure if he can even breathe. He doesn't push me away though, choosing instead to return the embrace and we stand in the small room, laced in each other's arms for what feels like a blissful eternity and I am reminded of the one, beautiful, perfect night we spent together, our last in ROC.

Then I feel his fingertips on my chin. He lifts my head and kisses me, soft and slow and sweet, in the way that makes my knees melt and my stomach flip-flop with giddy joy. It's the way old Rey kissed me when we thought we'd never see each other again and now I realize how horribly I have missed him.

Pulling slightly away, he takes my shoulders in his hands, running his fingers across my collarbone and up my neck until he cups my face.

"Kelsey, I swore to myself I wouldn't do this, that I wouldn't beg you, but I can't hold true to that anymore. Please... please choose me. Please tell me you love me and that you'll pick me over Jax. If you do, I promise I'll forget ROC. I'll help you convince Nole and Charlie to get everyone to run away. Or you and I will just run away and leave all this behind, whatever you want. *Please.* All I really need is you."

This is my Rey, the Rey who would always give up anything for me. And selfishly, I have always accepted it, never fully realizing what I was doing to him.

I break away, twisting my face to hide my own tears. I've spent so much time crying. I don't want to anymore and yet it takes all the strength I have to keep the tears away.

"Kelsey, please."

"No, Rey. This isn't fair. I do love you and you know that, but you can't make those kinds of promises just to convince me to be with you. You'll never be able to forget about ROC. After everything you just said minutes ago, I know you Rey. I know you can't move on from this. I hate my father and the other Councilmembers for what they've done, but for you, it's been so much more. They destroyed my trust, but for you, they've destroyed your entire life."

"What are you saying?" he asks.

I face him again, hating what I'm about to say next but knowing there's no other way around it. Rey has always had the ability to do that, change my mind without even meaning to. It's how I always ended up in trouble when we were kids. I have no illusions that it won't end any differently now.

"I won't help you break into or attack ROC," I say. "But I won't stop you nor will I hold it against you if that is the choice you make. This has changed you, made you into someone else who I don't even recognize. Regardless of Jax, or me and Jax or however that ends up, I want my best friend back. If this is the only option we have, then so be it."

He goes to open his mouth, but I hold up a hand.

"Don't say anything. This doesn't mean I've picked you over Jax and it doesn't mean I've made a decision. What happens between you and me is totally separate from what happens to you and ROC."

Chewing his lips, he swallows and then stares at me hard. "And what happens if I kill your father?"

My gaze drops to the floor. I have no idea how to answer. A part of me wants the man to pay for what he's done, the lives he's destroyed and for letting my mother be killed, but the other part reminds me this man is my father. He raised me and loved me and has probably been devastated since I disappeared.

"That's what I thought," is all Rey says when I don't respond. "Our lives will never be separate from ROC."

I raise my eyes, finding his. "Do whatever you need to do Rey. Whatever you think is best for you. Then we can worry about us."

CHAPTER NINETEEN

Three days have passed since Sawyer died and Elijah disappeared. I can't say I haven't spent most of that time looking over my shoulder expecting to see Elijah's fiery hair and maniacal eyes behind me. The nightmares won't stop and I feel bad because I've been sleeping at Jax's bedside and my screams wake him every night when all he really needs is rest.

He doesn't want me to leave though, and at least he's showing slow improvement. Color has returned to his skin and yesterday he sat up and ate an entire bowl of soup and some bread. Even the fever has broken and his wounds no longer look so wicked and inflamed. We haven't been able to move him from the safe house yet, but maybe in a few more days when he's stronger.

I haven't spoken to Rey since our fight, or whatever it was. Not so much because we are avoiding each other, but because he's spent so much time with Nole and Charlie plotting against ROC. I would have thought they'd need some down time to recover from our war with the League rather than race straight into another one, but both Rey and Nole have launched themselves into these plans with intense vigor, surviving off the adrenaline from our recent win. I think Charlie trails along so as not to be left in the dark, or perhaps to provide a voice of reason. She hasn't been the same since... well, since we ended the League.

I know little of the plans, holding to my promise to not be involved but to not pass judgment on Rey or anyone else. I have no desire to ask questions and have found it's easier to not judge when I don't know anything. Besides, Rey needs this, maybe Nole and Charlie and the rest of the Risers do too.

And for the time being, Jax needs me. Camrie, the closest person to a doctor we have on the surface, came from the Riser's compound to tend to the wounded. She checks on Jax often, but others were wounded in the battle whom she needs to attend to as well.

"Are you hungry?" I ask Jax after changing the bandage wound around his chest for the third time.

"Not really."

His response worries me because he should be hungry and the fact he isn't means his body could still be fighting a deep infection we don't know about.

I brush his arm. "You should at least try to eat something. I can see if there's fresh bread downstairs? I heard someone talking about making some."

He thinks for a moment, as if assessing his stomach.

"For me?" I plead.

Smiling weakly, he nods. "Ok. I can eat a little."

Standing from the side of the bed, I touch his hand for a moment. "I'll be right back."

Gripping my fingers, he flashes a charming grin. "And I'll be here looking fabulous."

Making my way to the old kitchen, I accidently startle Charlie as she heads out, a loaf of warm, fresh bread in her hands. The delicious smell floats from inside the kitchen, indicating additional loaves await. My mouth waters.

"Kelsey, how's Jax?" Charlie asks. "I feel bad I haven't really been up to check on him the last few days."

"He's better, sleeps mostly so aside from the occasional

ridiculous joke, you really aren't missing much."

"I know, but I should make a better effort. He's grown up into a good young man, hard to believe he was that anxious, panicked, silent twelve-year old that showed up at the compound all those years ago. It's so sad about Daniel, I still have a hard time accepting he's gone. Jax needed a father figure. A mother figure too, though that never really worked out. I thought of him as a son once, but..."

Her voice fades off as we both stand in awkward silence. I haven't told anyone, Rey or Jax included, what I learned the night we ended the League. I don't think Ryder or Nole or anyone else who had been there has said a word of it either. It's not our secret to tell.

Still, I hadn't expected Charlie to ever mention it, let alone talk about it, but here she stands, her brownish-green eyes hidden as she gazes at the floor. She looks thinner, weaker, exhausted; less like the confident leader who strode into that cabin prison my first morning on the surface accusing me of being a spy.

"You must think I'm a horrible person," she says.

"I... me? What?" I stammer. "No. I think you're amazing. You've saved my life, what, three times now?"

"I know. It always seemed the right thing to do, but I've begun to wonder if I put more people at risk to save one life because I seem to think it will make up for what I've done."

The sadness hanging on her voice tears at my gut as she slumps into an old, dusty armchair placed against the scratched and marred wood-paneled wall.

"It wasn't always like this. Sawyer wasn't always so... so psychotic. He was actually a really good father when I was a child. He loved his family and the rest of the League and was grooming me to take over his role someday because he believed

I was a natural born leader, even over my brothers."

"Then, when I was fifteen, ROC attacked the League with some sort of biologically engineered virus. We lost half our people, my mother and both older brothers included. Sawyer sat at their bedside, watching them gasp for air as the virus essentially drowned them in their own mucus. So many died in those couple months that we ended up just making a mass grave instead of burying each person individually. I still remember the smell of it."

I say nothing. I know my father had no involvement in that attack. He wouldn't have even been appointed to the council at that time, let alone be Protector, but guilt chews on me all the same.

"After they died," Charlie continues, "Sawyer fell apart, transformed into this insane tyrannical force intent on destroying ROC and everyone inside. Over the years, he tried dozens of ways to get through that door or draw people out, all of which failed obviously, and drove him even deeper into insanity each time. It was like he deemed each failed attempt a personal attack on himself, as if that stupid door were taunting him."

"Then one day about twenty years ago I guess, a ROC escapee showed up looking for help. They shot him, right in the head outside the main doors. But it gave Sawyer his next insane idea. He ordered his men to search for any other ROC citizens who may have escaped with the belief that if we captured enough and held them for a fake ransom, ROC would fling open their doors to retrieve their lost citizens. He's been set on that course for decades now, I can't even imagine how many prisoners have died in that time. He always thought he just needed *one more*. One more and then it would be good enough. As you know, it would never work. I told Sawyer that too, that his idea was hopeless. He hit me for the first time ever in my life. Smacked me right across the face with the back of his hand and knocked me flat to the floor. But it wasn't even so much that he had hit me, but the look on his face when he did it, as if I were the enemy. I knew if I ever dared to stand in front of him or derail his mission, he'd kill me without a second thought. That's when I knew I had to leave."

"That was easier said than done though. At that point I was married and Elijah was already four. I wanted to take him with me so badly. I had to save my only child from the madness of my family and whatever war would inevitably begin between the League and ROC. I thought if I could just get us both far enough away, Elijah would stand a chance to grow up normal. I thought we'd go east. Some people say there's a huge ocean there and I always wanted to see it for myself."

She falls into a silence so long, I wonder if she's forgotten she's been speaking aloud all this time. I don't press though, wanting to hear the full story, try to understand how Elijah came to be so awful, but I don't want to push Charlie away. I have no idea why she's chosen now to confide in me.

Charlie scratches at her face, maybe trying to discreetly brush tears away from her sunken eyes. "I had a whole plan and I didn't tell anyone, not even Elijah. We'd sneak out in the middle of the night and head into the woods and never look back. I knew how to survive, how to hunt and trap and build shelter, Sawyer insisted he raise strong, independent children."

"Except somehow my husband found out. Maybe I was careless with a small detail, or he noticed me acting strangely, I'll never know. He was my father's first in command and held more loyalty to Sawyer than he ever did for me. Sometimes I wonder if Sawyer pressured the marriage so my husband could keep watch on me. I don't know. Either way, they took Elijah and locked me in the basement. They said I'd be hung for treason like the United States use to do right before the revolution and all the bombs."

"So how did you escape?" I ask, unable to hold my silence any longer.

"With Daniel's help," she says to my surprise. "They had him locked up down there too. We escaped together and ran into the woods. After a couple days we happened upon the compound, abandoned and in a serious state of disrepair at the time. For some reason, Sawyer's men never came looking in those first few years. I guess he figured I'd run in fear and he was never interested in anyone who showed fear. He had Elijah to raise and groom anyway. As long as I didn't bother him, I thought I could finally live in peace. Daniel and I started to fix up the buildings and eventually others from various parts of the country showed up, a sort of collection of nomads and misfits who belonged nowhere else. The compound grew and they became my family, but I've never been able to forgive myself for leaving Elijah behind, seeing the... the monster my husband and my father turned him into. If I had just tried-"

"You did try," I insist, lightly touching her arm in reassurance. "You tried to save him, it's Sawyer who corrupted him."

She rubs at her forehead, as if the painful memories have manifested into a migraine. "I should have stayed. I shouldn't have planned to run away."

"You think things would have ended any differently?"

Looking away, she wipes at her face again and I wish I had a tissue or handkerchief or something but things like that don't exist on the surface.

"Maybe it would have been different," she says. "Maybe it would have ended the same. We'll never know, will we? I just can't believe I left my baby behind to become... what he is."

"Charlie," I say, resting a hand on hers. "You can't be responsible for what others become. Even with what you endured, you're still a good person who does good things. Maybe Elijah didn't have good role models or a fair chance as a kid, but eventually we all learn the difference between right and wrong and you can't tell me no matter how he was brain-washed that

Elijah believes torture and murder is a good thing. At some point we all have to make a choice. Ryder said to me once that 'we choose who we become'. You choose to leave and turn your back on your father and his insanity. Elijah, even once he was old enough to know better, choose differently. There's nothing you could have done after that."

A sad smile hovers on her lips. Then she sighs as if coming to terms with what is and shoving aside the thoughts of what could have been. "Thank you, Kelsey. I mean it. You're a good person, you know how to inspire hope. I think that's why I admire you so much."

I blink. "You admire me?"

"Of course. To have survived what you have? Escape your father's rule, run away from your home, try so hard to keep others safe regardless of harm to yourself? That all takes a very unique kind of strength and courage. I would know. It's a kind that can't be taught or forced upon someone. It's the kind that comes from inside your soul, a part of who you are as much as your eye color or curly hair. Our lives are so very similar; I think that's why I've always liked you and why I've risked so much to keep you safe from my father. I guess I've always felt like I was saving a part of myself too. Or maybe saving someone else's child because I couldn't save my own."

Leaning forward in her chair, she pulls me into a hug and after a moment of surprise, I return the embrace, reminded again of how she smells and feels like the few memories I have of my mother. I wish I knew what it was like to grow up with a mom, to have someone to aspire to be. I guess Maeva and Elsa and now Charlie are the closest I will be fortunate enough to have had.

A moment later Charlie pulls away, her calm, unflappable mask back in place. She rises from the chair, runs a hand through her hair and turns to leave.

"Hey Charlie," I call, causing her to twist back around. "Just out of curiosity, why was Daniel locked up too? I didn't know he'd been part of the League. I guess I don't know anything about him at all really."

She shakes her head. "I don't know why Sawyer had him as a prisoner, he'd never talk about it. Guess now we'll never know. He did have a family though, in the League. A wife and a little girl about nine or ten at the time. He never talked much about either of them, I think it was too painful, but I do remember him saying his daughter, Lillynn I think her name was, was a real spunky kid."

Charlie's gone around the corner of the hall before her words finally settle in my mind. Then another set of words float to the forefront of my memory.

I dunno. I guess I just didn't expect someone being forced to conform to ROC rules to be so spunky. You remind me of someone I used to know.

Lillynn. I'd reminded Daniel of his daughter, the daughter he'd left behind so he too could survive against the League. That's why Daniel allowed me to live in his home, why he stood up for me and protected me until the end. Like Charlie was trying to save herself through me, Daniel was trying to save his daughter.

I wonder if it helped him find some closure at all. I don't know. I don't know what people think and feel as they lay dying, what parts of their life suddenly make perfect sense and what questions will forever go unanswered. I kind of hope I never do know. When I die, which seems to be a growing possibility each day I walk the surface, I want it to be quick and painless. I don't want time to examine my mistakes or relive lost moments and memories. I just want to be gone.

But Charlie's conversation, learning her and Daniel's past, does leave me wondering about mine. If Rey's plan is successful, my father will die and ROC will become a memory, a thing of my past. I hate it and hate everything it stands for, but once upon a time, it was my home.

Forgetting why I even came downstairs in the first place, I rush back down the hallway in search of Rey.

CHAPTER TWENTY

I find Rey in the dining room where I met with Charlie the day she told me the truth about ROC, appropriate I guess for the next words coming out of my mouth.

"I want to go back to the O.Z."

Rey twists around slowly in his chair, his face knotted in confusion. "What?"

"I want to go back to ROC. I mean, not inside obviously, I think the walls would suffocate me at this point, but I want you to show me where you escaped from. I want to… I don't know, say good-bye I guess before you and Nole and Charlie blow it up or whatever you're planning."

"We're not blowing it up," he says, returning to his drawings as if my request is a joke not to be taken seriously. Ancient, laminated maps and dry, crinkled papers litter the table, rustling as Rey pokes through them before finding one he needs.

"Fine," I say with slightly more command in my voice. "But I want to see it, where you escaped, I mean."

Again, he shifts to face me, head cocked to one side so locks of hair flop over his forehead. "Why?"

"I don't know. I can't explain it, I just feel like I need to."

Sitting back in his chair and stretching, he sighs. "Fine, but not today, Nole and I are supposed to go over these notes." He waves at rolls of yellowed paper with hand-drawn lines and notations.

"Is that ROC?" I ask, stepping closer to catch a glimpse of

his work.

"Yeah. The air ducts mostly. Or what I can remember of them anyway. Where we can enter, where the main ones go, how to get out. I'm trying to overlay it with these maps of the surface to get an idea of how big everything is, maybe find other external vents if any exist. I'm not sure how accurate any of it will be since I left, but it's the best I can do."

There must be two dozen renderings spread along the table, some showing specific details such as air vents, camera locations, how many feet span between each.

"You did all this from memory?"

His shoulders shrug, as if it's not that big a deal. "It was my job for several years."

He looks so tired, dark circles hanging under blood-shot eyes. I wonder how late he stays up each night to do this, sitting alone in the old dining room pulling this information from the depths of his memories. I've been so worried about Jax I haven't even considered that Rey needs someone looking after him too.

"Rey, this is more than just job knowledge," I say, picking up one of the drawings that details the vents running outside the Council Chambers. Arrows mark which ones run into the Chambers and each shaft has numerical notations indicating width and whether or not someone could fit inside.

"I thought you didn't want to be involved in this?" He doesn't snap, but a subtle note of annoyance hangs in his voice.

I put the drawing back down. "I don't. This just seems like... a lot. More than you would have known for work."

"It's part of Jericho's plan. Or well, the plan of whoever is leading the revolutionaries. They asked me to map the ductwork because it will give them access to the Councilmembers' suites and the Council Circle, even the Gendarme's armory. I've been doing it for years. I had to be secretive about it though.

Can't have the Gendarme seeing me wander around with expensive tablets or measuring distances between the cameras."

"That's why you learned to write. To take notes, create these drawings once before."

He nods. "I wrote on little scrapes stuffed into my sleeves. That way, if anyone got suspicious or I was caught, I could eat the paper and get rid of the evidence."

I think about the frayed ends of the sleeves of Rey's coveralls. I always assumed he tugged on them because they were too short when all this time he was probably trying to keep slips of paper hidden inside, afraid one would fall out.

Rey sits back in his chair. "Jericho didn't want to risk someone hacking into an electronic device, or risk the possibility the Gendarme already controls all the electronics anyway, so we write everything out. He's been making paper in his suite out of old pieces of linen, trash, food containers, stuff like that and keeping everything hidden. Some in his suite, some spread out in the suites of the other leaders so that if anyone gets caught, the whole mission isn't lost."

"How long?" I ask.

"What do you mean?"

"How long have people been planning a revolution?"

"I don't know, I only got involved last year but for Jericho and the others? Years. Maybe even a decade. It's a gentle thing, revolutions are. If one person gets caught, it puts everyone at risk. If the entire mission doesn't go exactly as planned, there's no second chance. He needs enough people to believe him, and be willing to fight, to outnumber the Gendarme. He needs a little spark, something to ignite the whole thing and energize everyone in the Subs. Once that happens, once enough believe in the cause and believe in life on the surface, the Gendarme will be useless."

We stand in silence for several moments. I gaze over the drawings, the tangible outcome of years of Rey's life and the hopes of so many people. And I had no idea. If I hadn't known the truth about the surface, if I believed the lies of my father and the Councilmembers, what side of the revolution would I have fought on?

"Can we go tomorrow then?" I ask eventually, pulling my gaze from the maps and drawings.

"Sure. We'll have to leave in the morning to make it back before dark."

"Then I'll see you outside in the morning. I'll bring lunch."

Leaving, I tug the dining room door shut behind me leaving Rey to his work.

As I turn in the hallway, I'm surprised to see Evy coming down the main staircase, one hand on the railing and the other supporting her brother.

"Evy, Randolph," I say and both look up. Randolph's face is still adorned with the markings from Elijah and the rest of the League. He favors his left ankle, leaning onto Evy as they ascend the last few steps.

"Hey," Evy says with a smile.

I nod to Randolph, offering an encouraging smile of my own. "It's nice to see you walking around."

He grimaces. "I would hardly call this walking. Camrie says it's just badly sprained but I swear it feels broken. If it weren't for Evy acting as a crutch, I'd still be confined to bed."

"Camrie says it will be good for him to move around some."

"Hey, Kelsey," Randolph says, "I didn't thank you yet. Evy filled me in. And Rey. What you did, what everyone here did. I don't know how to repay you." Tears fill his eyes and he doesn't bother to hide them.

My fingertips graze his arm in comfort. "You saved me first, remember? Now we're even. I'll forgive you for shooting me too."

He laughs. "But you aren't going to let me forget, huh?"

"No, that's just crazy talk now."

"We're going outside for some fresh air," Evy says. "Want to join?"

I shake my head. "No, I'm alright. I'll catch you both later."

They slowly head for the door, Randolph attempting to bear more of his own weight as his sister hovers nearby, ready to catch him if he falters.

I don't know what to do for the rest of the day. Rey has to plan, Jax has to sleep and Nadia's still back at the Risers' compound. I hope she's ok and that someone's told her Jax and I are alive. I imagine that wolf hasn't left her side.

Jax. I was supposed to bring him food. That was probably an hour ago. Making my way back to the kitchen, I find one last loaf of bread, some berries from the woods and a bucket of fresh water. Gathering the food and filling a chipped china bowl with water, I return to Jax's room.

He sits up, gingerly, but without grimacing in pain this time; a huge improvement over a few days ago.

"Did you find the kitchen by way of the old compound?" he asks.

"Sorry. I got caught up with Charlie."

"She just left. Wanted to see how I'm feeling."

"They're planning an attack on ROC," I blurt out. I debated whether or not I should tell him, but he'll find out sooner or later. Secrets help no one.

Sitting straighter, his eyes sparkle as the corners of his lips turn upward. "Awesome. Let's go."

I put a hand to his chest, pressing him back to the pillows. "They aren't going now. They need an actual plan. A good one. This isn't going to be like our attacks on the League. ROC is made out of cement, cinderblock and steel. Fireworks will only do so much damage down there."

"We're out of fireworks anyway."

"So then they really need a good plan."

"Who's in charge? I want in."

"Of course you do. God forbid you don't run straight into danger every time it presents itself."

"You're one to talk. And what fun would running *from* danger be anyway?"

"Nole's in charge. And Charlie of course."

Lifting his eyebrows, Jax pulls his mouth into a tight line. "And Rey."

Not a question.

I collapse into the chair I've been sleeping in ever since we arrived at the safe house.

"Jax," I say, exhaustion wearing heavy in my voice. "I know you don't like Rey but-"

"See, that's the thing," Jax says, cutting me off and propping himself up on his good arm. "I do like him. I think, given different circumstances, he and I would be really good friends. And the fact I actually like him, makes me want to dislike him even more, if that makes any sense at all. I guess that's why you have such a hard time deciding, but if you picked him over me, I'd understand. I'd get it. He might not be as smart as me, or nearly as handsome, but he's a good guy, a good friend and I know he loves you."

With a wince, Jax slides across the bed to move closer to me. "What I hate is not knowing. I hate lying up here in this stupid bed not knowing what's happening, what you're think-ing, how this is going to end. That's what I can't stand, all the uncertainty."

I can't look at him, I'm too ashamed. He speaks the painful truth, I'll never deny it, but hearing the words from his mouth confirming the ones screaming inside my brain makes what I've done, what I continue to do, so much worse.

"I'm sorry, Jax," I whisper, gaze still tracing the floor-boards. "I'll tell you the same thing I told Rey. Too much has happened too quickly and while the League is gone, we still aren't finished the war. Not with Elijah still out there. I won't decide anything now, I can't. Right now, we all need to focus on surviving, then we can worry about a future, whatever future that might be."

He says nothing for so long, I think he's fallen back asleep, but when I lift my eyes, Jax stares out the window, though I don't think it's the fluffy white clouds he sees.

"Fine," he mumbles. Then, with another pained grimace, he rolls over and pulls the blanket up to his ear, signaling I am no longer welcome here.

I rise from the chair, feeling like my stomach has dropped onto the floor. I don't know what to say so I say nothing at all, pushing myself to the door before either of us say something we regret.

Upon reaching the threshold, I pause, one hand on the doorframe because otherwise I might fall over from the emo-tions raking my insides. "I'm going to ROC tomorrow morning, to the air vent where Rey escaped. And Rey is going with me. I want to, I don't know, say good-bye or something. I just thought you should know."

And then I leave him alone to sit in pain, half of which I've caused and none that I can remedy.

CHAPTER TWENTY- ONE

As promised, I exit the main doors of the school building just in time to see the sun peek over the horizon, tingeing the night sky with the first burgundy- gold splashes of morning. A pack of food and water canteens hang over my shoulder.

A shuffling of footsteps meets my ears and I turn to find Rey, the sight of him easing away a tension I didn't know I had.

"What?" he asks when he notices my expression, "you didn't think I'd come?"

"I don't know what to think about anything anymore. You ready?"

"That depends, what's in that lunch bag?"

I grin. "Sandwiches, some pears, a couple oranges, water."

"And?"

"And I snuck some of those buttermilk biscuits that I'm pretty sure you've been single-handedly polishing off."

"That's my girl," he says, tugging on one of my loose curls and letting it bounce free from his fingertips. Then he points over the tree tops. "We're heading that way. And I hope you've got on your hiking boots."

* * *

As the day unfolds, clouds roll in and a grey sky follows our journey, threatening rain but never quite following through. Still, the ominous tone, the heavy, muggy air and the stillness of the woods unsettles me, as if more than just the potential weather means us harm. I startle and look over my shoulder so many times, Rey eventually walks behind me, calling out changes in direction and giving me a small sense of comfort that someone watches my back.

With no sun to track thanks to the thick clouds, I'm not sure what time it is when we reach a small clearing and pause.

"There is it," Rey says.

"Where?" I ask, craning my neck and squinting my eyes, searching the trees, tall grass, dancing wildflowers and scattered boulders. Nothing seems out of the ordinary. "I don't see anything."

"I think that's the point."

Stepping ahead, Rey hoists himself onto one of the largest rocks, then turns and offers me his hand. Clasping it, I'm hauled upward onto the rock as well, pebbles and loose stones shifting under my boots. Rey kneels down and brushes away fresh moss and dead leaves. As he does so, a rusted metal door appears, no larger than four feet square and set down into the rock so that unless one happens to be standing on top of it and knows what to look for, it would never be found. The hinges are broken, probably from when Rey exited.

"Wow," I breathe, voice low.

"You don't have to whisper," Rey says with a chuckle. "ROC is still two miles down and I'm sure the gas chamber is closed and empty right now."

"I can't believe you climbed all that to come out here."

"Neither can I."

I look up at him, catching those blue eyes so familiar I know them better than my own. "Did you expect all of this when you got to the surface?"

"Did you?" he asks with a forlorn grin. Looking around, I take in the trees and the rocks and the sky and all the things that, once upon a time, I never thought I'd see. I never even dared to believe some of it could exist. Now here we are, and none of it has been what I expected that moment I stepped out of ROC.

"Is there anything else you wanted to see before we head back?" he asks.

I already know the answer, but it still takes me a moment to respond. "No. I guess I just wanted to see it with my own eyes."

"Oh, dear Kels, all these years and you still can't take my word for it."

"Oh yeah? What happened to the cameras in Sector B on my birthday?"

With an impish, sideways smirk Rey scratches his head. "Sector B cameras. On your birthday, you say? I don't recall."

"They were broken, conveniently where you know I like to go read."

"Oh, *those* cameras. I climbed up into the vent and disabled them that morning. Temporarily of course. How else was I going to give you your birthday present?"

"You mean a stolen cookie?"

"I prefer confiscated."

"And you wonder why I can't take your word for it."

"You ready to go back? We're probably going to have to walk the last mile or two in the dark."

I take another look at the old, worn door, the only sign of an entire civilization two miles below filled with tens of thousands of people living in fear and believing the world above is nothing but a radioactive, barren wasteland. It makes me want to scream down the air shaft that the life they know is a lie. I want to rip the metal covering off and fling myself back into ROC and rescue all those innocent people and hold every last Councilmember accountable for their crimes. Punish them for murder.

But I'm too scared. I'm leaving Rey and Charlie and Nole to do what I can't bring myself to handle.

"When?" I ask softly.

Rey doesn't answer and I think he hasn't heard my question, but when I lift my head I see him staring intently at me.

"I'm not sure. Not soon. We need more time to prepare and we need to get back to the Riser's compound to train anyone going with us. They'll need to be familiar with the inside of ROC, how to maneuver through the air shafts, a general idea of layout. And, you know, allow time for everyone to recover from our battle with the League. Maybe by the end of the summer, maybe longer."

"It'll be before the next Gamble though, right?"

"I think so."

"Can you promise? Promise you'll do whatever it takes to make sure ROC never holds another Gamble?"

Moving closer, Rey cups my face in both hands, his eyes gazing deep into mine. I can see his jaw twitch, his expression serious and stern. "I promise. There will never be another Gamble in this world."

Lacing my arms around him, we stand together on the boulder inches from the nearest ROC air shaft, locked in our embrace, a repeat of a month ago and two miles down before our lives changed so radically.

"Are you ready to go back now?" he whispers into my ear.

I nod and pull away, jumping off the rock and landing on

the pine-needled earth. Rey follows and steers me back the direction we came, winding our way through the trees and shrubs.

"Do you remember when we were kids," he begins, "and we used to pretend we were on the surface?"

"When we'd take all those fake, plastic plants in my suite and arrange them like a forest around the living room?"

"Yeah. And then we use to lay on the floor and stare up through the leaves and talk about how we were going to be the first generation in a century to walk on the earth again."

"Well, I guess we kind of got some of it correct."

He laughs. "Yeah. I just honestly never thought those dreams would come true, and now here we are. I wish I could go back to my ten-year old self and tell him to be patient."

"I wish I could go back to my ten-year old self and tell her the truth. Then we could have runaway to the surface together when we were kids and never had to sit through another Gamble."

"It's strange though," Rey says, "when you think about it. As awful as the Gamble is, had my number never been called, we wouldn't be here now. We'd be in ROC, probably getting married or something, but we certainly wouldn't be breathing fresh air and enjoying this grey, overcast afternoon."

I think about this statement for a moment. I hate the Gamble, always have, always will, but in a way, in spite of everything the Gamble has taken from us, it has also set us free. A part of me has to at least appreciate that much. I guess even the worst things in life have some good quality hidden somewhere. Like Ryder said, you can't paint the world with black and white.

* * *

While we never had the chance to see the sun today, we still know when it sets, the forest falling into deep, navy shadows and eventually heavy darkness. We brought lanterns with us just in case, but with the clouds blocking any moonlight, the lanterns only offer so much visibility through the trees. We slow our last mile, taking careful steps on our way back to the safe house. One misstep could be a broken ankle.

Keeping my eyes on the almost indistinguishable trail and unsuccessfully attempting to dodge thorny branches and low tree limbs, I don't see what I smack into. Something hard whacks into my face, reeling me backward as I grapple for my gun.

"What the-?" Rey barks, running into me from behind.

But I'm rooted to the spot, the lantern hanging in my outstretched arm and my other hand halfway to my weapon. My mouth gapes open, eyes wide and heart stopped as I stare in horror at the object dangling before me. I rest a hand on it to stop it from swinging into my face.

Then I see another, and another and as I turn, I realize that someone littered this entire section of the forest with the macabre display. Someone who knows where the safe house is. Someone who knew I left this morning and which way I'd be returning.

Someone who was following me and who created this grotesque scene with the sole intent of rattling my bones and slithering under my skin, a game of psychological terror.

The nauseating, metallic smell of blood hits the back of my nostrils, causing me to gag.

"What are they?" Rey asks with noted disgust, taking in the presentation.

"Mannequins," I choke, bile rising in my throat. "They're Sawyer's mannequins."

And they are. Dozens of them. All with their heads removed, strung up by their ankles to hang from the trees. All of them covered in blood.

CHAPTER TWENTY-TWO

"We have to leave!" I command, barging into the dining room where Nole and Charlie pour over Rey's drawings. "Now!"

Stunned at my entrance, both glance up in confusion.

"It's Elijah," I say, my voice on the edge of tears I'm desperately hoping to keep at bay. Along with the panic. If I give in to either and allow myself to fall apart, I'm not sure how long it will take for me to piece myself together again. "He's here somewhere, hiding in the woods."

They lurch to their feet, Charlie's face going pale and Nole's brow furrowing until his eyes look like tiny bits of black coal stuck to his face.

"How do you know?" Charlie asks. "Did you see him?"

"It's the mannequins," I say. "Almost thirty of them, hanging in the forest less than a quarter mile away. He's chopped off all the heads and covered them in what I am really, really hoping is animal blood."

I know Charlie understands what I mean. I bet those plastic statues haunt her dreams the way they haunt mine. I've already explained to Rey and am prepared to explain to Nole before he speaks.

"We'll double the guard, triple if we have to. We can send a team to go back to our compound and gather more men."

"We have to leave," I protest.

He shakes his head. "We can't. There are eight people here injured from the battle, Jax included, who aren't well enough to travel yet. I know the compound isn't more than a day's hike, but some of them can't even walk down the stairs unaided. I won't risk their health."

"So you'll risk their lives?"

Nole tilts his head and subtly raises an eyebrow. "I am not ensuring further damage to their health on the possibility of one man causing more trouble."

"Then Kelsey needs to go," Rey says. "He's after her more than anyone else."

"No! I'm not leaving everyone I care about behind."

"Seriously, Kels, you're going to argue about this? He wants to kill you. Not Jax or Randolph or anyone else here. *You.*"

"I'm not leaving without everyone here. God knows what Elijah will do if he gets into the safe house and doesn't find me."

"She's right," Nole says. "I'm not sending our injured members on a trek through the woods, but there's also no predicting what he'll do next. I'm sorry to say this in your presence, Charlie, but Elijah is completely unhinged."

Charlie drops her head, long auburn hair concealing her face. She slumps back into her chair, shoulders sagging as she runs a trembling hand over her face. I know she agrees with Nole, but she'll never voice it aloud and condemn her own son. I can't say I blame her. I never wanted to acknowledge my father's heinous crimes out loud. Doing so makes it more real than I still want to admit.

However, none of that changes the fact that Elijah is a psychopath and that he has fixed all this hatred and rage on me. But I'm not leaving. I can't leave Rey and Jax behind. Or Charlie or anyone else while knowing Elijah stalks the woods. Nor will

I lead him to Nadia and the other Risers. He's already made it very clear with his display tonight in the woods, where I go, he will follow. And I know he'll kill anyone who stands in his way.

"Then what do you propose we do?" demands Rey with a scowl.

Nole rubs his chin, fresh stubble scratching against his fingers. "We wait. He's one man. We can put together a small army by tomorrow night. I'd like to see him try to get through our defenses when he has none himself."

"So we're using Kelsey as bait again?"

"Elijah has already decided she's bait. At least we have the advantage of knowing what he wants and where she is. So, on that note," Nole says turning to me, "I'm putting you under constant guard. I doubt he'll attack tonight and that will buy us time to get additional reinforcements if you're insistent on staying here."

"I'm insistent."

"Then in the meantime, you don't go anywhere, inside this house or otherwise, without both your weapon and an additional armed companion."

"That sounds miserable," I grumble. I've managed to escape the confines of both ROC and the League only to lose my freedom once again.

"It's better than dead," says Charlie, her tone emotionless and face blank. Then she stalks from the room and into the darkness of the halls. Nole stares after her, his face masked with concern. As I observe him, his emotions for Charlie so evident on his features he might as well have written there, it's the first time I realize he's perhaps in love with her.

"She's right," he adds. "I don't care if it's Rey or even Jax with you as long as he's well enough and you're both inside the house. Or me even if necessary, but that's an order. Understand?"

I don't like it, but it is better than dead, so I grit my teeth and nod.

"Fine," Rey says, "then I'm playing watchdog first, ok?"

"I'd be shocked if you didn't volunteer first," Nole replies, the weariness heavy on his voice. "It's been a long day. You're safe here for now. I suggest you both get some sleep."

As Rey and I leave the dining room and head for the main staircase; a wide, ornate, wooden behemoth of thick treads, carved railings and what I think was once burgundy carpet. It twists around the entry hall and up into the second and third floors of the mansion.

"I should let Jax know I'm back," I say.

"Are you going to tell him about Elijah?"

"I don't know. I guess I'll see what sort of shape he's in."

Climbing the stairs to the second level, I veer right toward Jax's room, Rey on my heels. I give him a weird look. "You're coming with me?"

Jerking a thumb at his puffed-out chest, his face grows overly serious. "Bark. Or something like that. Watch dog, remember?"

I roll my eyes. "Ugh, fine."

Peeking around Jax's door, I see him sprawled on the bed, arms and legs spread wide and mouth hanging open.

"Maybe you should leave him a note?" Rey suggests.

"I don't know how to write. Nor do we have anything to write with."

Rey surveys the room. "Ok, then hold on, I'll be *write* back."

I groan at the lame joke even though it elicits a small grin on my lips. "Clever. Aren't you supposed to be my guard and like, stay at my side every moment?"

"Elijah isn't in the house now and I'll only be a minute. Technically, you're with Jax right now, so he's currently your guard," Rey calls over his shoulder as he heads for the staircase. "And he's sleeping on the job. He should be ashamed of himself."

Shaking my head and smiling to myself, I quietly slip into Jax's room. Immediately I notice that he must have gotten out of bed earlier. The random assortment of antique objects on the dresser have been arranged into a neat row, all evenly spaced and placed shortest to tallest. The curtains on the windows have been adjusted so they are all open exactly the same amount. He even managed to move a small table and chair on the other side of the room to center them between two windows.

"Glad to see you're feeling better," I whisper, noting that more color graces his cheeks and he no longer wears beads of perspiration caused by the fever.

"Back," Rey announces softly, tip toeing up beside me. He places a yellowed, crumpled piece of paper on top of the dresser, scrawling a few words and then handing it to me.

Made it back safely. See you in the morning.

-Kelsey

"Thank you," I say, folding the paper and placing it on the night table sitting next to Jax's bed where he'll see it when he wakes up. Rey plops the pen beside it.

"He looks better," he says.

"Yeah. I think he's going to be ok."

"I'm still shocked he saved my life."

Nose wrinkling, I turn to gawk at Rey. "Why? Why wouldn't he?"

Rey thinks for a long time, eyes flicking over Jax's unconscious body. "Because I can't say I would have done the same for him. And I'm sorry because I know that makes me an awful person, and maybe, in the moment I really would have done the same thing he did without giving it a second thought, but when I think about it now, I don't know. It would be less... complicated if one of us had died. Then I hate myself for even thinking about that because the only person I actually want dead is Elijah."

At first, I'm shocked, then I'm furious that Rey could even think about wanting Jax dead, but when I see his face and how conflicted he is, I find my anger dissipating.

"You aren't a bad person, Rey. How many times did you have your name in the Gamble to help others? It's just your emotions. We all have to deal with them and even though they're sometimes illogical or even insane, they can still form decisions we make. That's how I ended up on the surface after all. Besides, I think you're right, if your roles had been reversed, in the chaos of the moment, you would have done the same thing Jax did. Like I've told you, I ometimes I wonder if you both aren't the same person separated into two different bodies."

Rey nods and presses his lips tight together. "Gross."

"Yeah ok, you ready for bed?'

"Extra ready. I am falling asleep standing here."

Making our way down the hall, Rey follows me to my own bedroom, smaller than Jax's with windows facing west. I'd prefer they face east because I want to see the sunrise every day, but as long as I can see the sky, I'm happy.

Flopping on a tattered sofa in one corner, Rey kicks his feet onto the armrest, wads a pillow under his head and shuts his eyes. I do the same, falling into my own bed. It's too warm for a blanket so I kick it off and close my eyes, listening to Rey's calm snores.

But I can't seem to fall asleep as easily as he did. Thoughts of Elijah scream through my brain. The fact that he found our safe house, he was less than a half mile away, the idea he could be prowling the woods, watching and waiting to make his next move.

I hate the man, but I'll give him credit for being smart. Whatever he plans, we won't see it coming, we can only hope we have enough manpower to stop him. Charlie and Nole will increase security and I have no doubt more Risers will arrive by tomorrow night, if not sooner depending on when Nole sends others to retrieve them. But will it be enough? Nole said that Elijah's just one man, which should make him easier to defeat, but one man is also a lot harder to catch.

I must fall asleep eventually though, because the next thing I know, I'm being gently shaken awake.

"Kelsey," a voice murmurs, a hand on my shoulder.

I blink, eyes needing a moment to adjust to the darkness filling the room. I must have only been asleep for a couple hours, the night only half over.

Rey is still collapsed on the far couch. Twisting my head, I look up to see Jax hovering over me. In the moonlight through the window over my head, I can see his eyes sunken from fatigue and stress, but his complexion slowly returning to normal.

"Jax? What's wrong? Do you feel ok?"

"Yes, yeah. I'm fine. Look, did you leave me this note?"

"What?"

"This? I just woke up and it was on my night table. Has your name at the bottom."

He holds out the note Rey wrote for me, still folded in half.

"Yeah. I didn't want to wake you up."

"What did you write?" he asks, blue-green eyes watching me carefully and I sense a hint of anxiety in his tone.

I sit even straighter, an uneasy churning in my gut. "Rey wrote it actually since I don't know how, but it said that I was home safe and I'd see you in the morning."

"Anything else?"

"No. I mean, my name, but that's it. Why? What's going on?"

Jax passes the note forward. I take it, my hands quivering slightly, and I inhale a tense breath. Sliding the page open, I squint to read it in the hints of moonlight from through the window. I see my original note, but below, written in a scrawl completely different from Rey's, someone has added:

PS- I'm watching you

Below are three sets of numbers. I don't recognize them right away, reading them a second time. When the realization of what they are sets in; the barcode numbers off of mine, Rey's and Jax's arms; and knowing the only way in which all could have been accurately obtained, I scream. An ear-splitting sound that vibrates through the house, loud enough to wake Sawyer's lifeless mannequins swinging from the forest trees.

CHAPTER TWENTY-THREE

"It doesn't change the fact that eight of our team can't travel," says Nole. He stands at the head of the massive dining room table, palms flat on its surface and head bowed. Spread around the table sit myself, Jax, Rey, Ryder, Camrie and two other people I recognize but whose names I'm unsure of. Candles and lanterns are dispersed through the space, creating more shadows than light in the large room. Given her relationship with Elijah, which is slowly making its way around the house, Charlie opted out of this meeting. Nole says its because she's too worried she can't be impartial. I think it's because she can't bear the thought of listening to our ideas around murdering her son.

"I hope you're not counting me in that eight?" Jax demands.

Lifting his sharp gaze, Nole fixes it on Jax. "I am because while you might be well enough to sit at this table, you still look like crap and couldn't possibly manage to hike through the woods given that you survived a near-fatal gunshot less than a week ago."

Sitting back against his chair, Jax folds his arms over his chest and scowls. "Even looking like crap I'm still the best-"

"Stop it," I hiss in his ear, leaning over the arm of my own seat and toward him. "This is serious. Don't go picking a battle of wills with Nole right now."

By the look on his face, which I have to agree has grown more pale and gaunt since earlier, I can tell he has some witty, ridiculous response clamoring around his brain, but he keeps his mouth shut.

"In theory, if we bring a few horses from our compound, we could move Jax as well as Colton and Prae," offers Camrie. "I checked on them this morning and they're probably stable and strong enough to ride that distance."

Nole shakes his head, standing to his full height. "That still leaves five who can't and I'm not leaving anyone behind after they were brave enough to face the League. The best place for those people is here and the best place for Kelsey is back at our compound where far more armed guards can watch out for her in a building we know how to defend."

"No," I say with as much command in my voice as I dare when addressing Nole.

"Kelsey," he says, "it's the safest place for you. There's nearly seven hundred people there, almost a hundred of them trained as guards. You'll be well protected."

"I'm not leading Elijah there to Nadia and all of those other people and children trying to live their lives. For all we know, he's waiting in the woods planning an ambush the moment we set foot into the forest. He might be nuts, but he's highly trained and I'm sure has a number of weapons and various traps at his disposal. He managed to get past our security, into this house and back out again without anyone noticing. He could be hiding in trees or under large rocks with a whole arsenal to take us out one by one."

"She's not wrong," mutters Jax with a shrug.

"So you suggest we wait here for him to pick us off one by one?" someone, a man with freckled skin and hair almost as vibrant as Elijah's, asks. "Like you said, he got into this house. Given how massive this place is, he could still *be* in here."

The idea makes my skin crawl and my eyes dart over the darkened corners of the room as if Elijah hides in one of them, watching me and waiting for me to be alone.

"Well," says Ryder, thick arms folded over his chest with his dirty boots propped up on the table, "this discussion can go round and round all day and get us nowhere, givin' Elijah more time to enact whatever that kid is plannin'."

"Agreed," admits Nole.

Ryder lowers his feet back to the floor with two thuds. Standing, he paces around the table with his hands clasped behind his back, muscles in his arms rippling. "We know he's after Kelsey and wherever she goes, he'll follow. We know he's got access to weapons; guns, grenades, whatever; and he may even have a person or two left from the League still standing beside him and helping. But we also know that he knows he's out-manned and out armed no matter which way he looks at it or how many weapons he's got at his disposal so whatever he plans, he's gonna be cautious. An ambush in the woods is a good idea, but at the end of the day, once we find that worm's hidin' spot, his game's over."

Nole scratches at his chin in thought. "Alright, what do you propose?"

"Tonight? Probably don't need to worry much. If he were gonna kill anyone he woulda done it while he was in here. Tomorrow? We take Kelsey back to the compound."

"I already said no!"

Ryder focuses his gaze on me, eyes like steel. "You're going. We can't protect you here and you're doin' nobody any favors by stayin'. We can take our risks in the woods, but I doubt he'll attack if we're in a large enough group. He wants to screw with your head first, then he wants to kill you. He can't do either of that if he ambushes us and risks the likely chance of gettin' himself killed."

"Doesn't matter, I don't want-"

Ryder's fist slams onto the table, cracking against the wood and causing everyone to jump. "This isn't about what you want! It's about keepin' you safe, the people here safe and endin' this once and for all!"

Whatever objections I had on my tongue, I clamp my mouth shut, startled by Ryder's outburst.

No one speaks for several seconds until Jax fake coughs. "When do we leave?"

"You aren't going anywhere," says Ryder. "You're not well enough."

Jax snorts. "Like hell."

"Jaxon, he's right," says Camrie. "I know you feel better, but that kind of travel, plus a potential fight with Elijah isn't safe for you right now."

"A fight with Elijah isn't exactly safe for anyone. Especially Elijah once I get my hands around his scrawny neck."

"You know what I mean."

Jax clenches his jaw, eyes narrowed. "Charlie has me in charge of security, so I feel like I get a say."

"Technically, I'm in charge of security. Charlie and I let you be in charge because I'm not gonna be around forever and need someone to take over, and you needed somethin' to keep you focused before you self-destructed. Right now, however, you're too emotionally involved and you're too injured, so I'm pullin' rank."

"But we need him," says Rey and I'm shocked he's actually vying for Jax to come with us. "He knows these woods better than almost anyone else except maybe you, Ryder. And he can fight well, even injured."

"Nice to see you both gettin' along, but you aren't comin'

either, kid," Ryder announces.

"Wait, what?" I sputter.

"They're stayin' here," the giant man repeats, his tone daring anyone to defy him. "Jax is too injured and Rey is needed here to continue to plan our infiltration of ROC with Charlie. World doesn't stop just cause Elijah's threatenin' you."

"I can plan the ROC stuff anywhere," says Rey. "Or it can just wait a few days. It's not like they're going anywhere any time soon."

"Not up for negotiation."

While he brings up valid points, especially with Jax's health, I question if there isn't more. I stare at each person in turn, Jax and Rey included. "Can Ryder and I have a moment?"

Camrie and the people whose names I still don't know, all seeming grateful for an excuse to escape, rise from the table and file out. Nole follows, sharing a knowing glance with Ryder before slipping into the hallway.

Jax and Rey don't move, both glaring at me with their arms crossed and faces marked with defiant challenge.

"Yes, of course, the one time you both actually get along is when you're arguing with me. Look, can Ryder and I just have a couple minutes alone to discuss all of this? I promise I'll come find both of you when we're finished."

They exchange a glance out of the corner of their eyes, Jax's jaw tight and Rey chewing on the inside of his mouth.

"Please?" I plead with a tone of frustration.

"Fine," grumbles Jax, pushing to his feet and stomping from the room.

"Rey?"

"I am going with you," he says, pointing a finger at me for

emphasis. "So whatever you both discuss, that better be part of the plan."

"Ok."

"Ok. Then I'll be upstairs in your room." He follows Jax's footsteps, shutting the door behind him.

I turn my attention to Ryder. "What's going on?"

"What'd you mean?"

"I mean, why don't you want them going?"

"Already told you."

"Sure. But I don't think that's the full truth and considering I'm at the center of this insanity, I want to know what's going on and why."

He sits forward in his chair to rest both elbows on the table. "Cause you love both of them and they love you. And right now, we don't have room for any of that. Jax got himself shot to impress you. I can't have that."

I balk. "Jax got himself shot to save Rey!"

"Yeah, cause he knows you love Rey and Jax loves you and now he's done somethin' noble and chivalrous or whatever. I've known that boy longer than you, he don't jump in front of bullets cause he wants to save lives."

"How can you say that?" I growl in disgust.

"Cause I know it's the truth."

"You're wrong about him."

"No. I'm not sayin' he knows the real reason behind his actions, colorful world, remember? But whatever the motives for that, I can't have those two riskin' their lives or the lives of others when we need to end this. And I need you focused cause Elijah's gonna have a good plan to get you and you need to be fully aware. If those boys are with us, you'll only worry about them and I don't want any of you doin' somethin' stupid."

"I'll worry about them regardless."

"You'll have less reason to worry with them here and safe."

"They'll follow us anyway."

"I'll put a couple guys here on watch. Have both boys locked up if we have to. Jax isn't gonna make it as far as he thinks he can anyway."

I stand, wandering to the row of windows overlooking the weed-choked front yard and into the woods beyond. The firelight from the lanterns behind me dances across the panes of glass as I gaze at the silent trees and dark sky. I wonder if Elijah's there now, watching the house, waiting for me to come out so he can put a bullet in my head. Or carve me up into tiny pieces.

I need to trust Ryder, probably more than anyone else right now. He's strong, smart, ready for a faceoff with a lunatic, and he's ruled purely by logic rather than emotion. I wouldn't say he's cold or careless, but I don't get the impression he has a lot of feelings to wade through before making decisions.

I hate the idea of going back to the Risers' compound without Jax and Rey, especially because we have no idea what Elijah will do next, but I can't deny the truth to Ryder's words. I've already sacrificed myself to save Jax and I'd do the same to save Rey. Who knows what either of them would do if my life were on the line, but it wouldn't necessarily be rational.

I close my eyes and face the facts. The best place for them, for anyone really, is as far away from me as possible right now. I need to do what is best for those I care about, which means, like Ryder said, I can't stay here.

Placing a hand on the dirty window, I rest my forehead against it. "When are we leaving?"

"First thing in the mornin', before Elijah can make a next

move. You should probably get some more sleep if you can."

"I want to kill him," I say.

"We will. We'll figure out a way."

"No. I want to be the one to actually do it."

He scratches at the stubble lining his jaw as a shimmer of candlelight reflects of his bald head. "Whatever happens, happens. I'm not gonna risk Elijah escapin' just so you can kill him."

"Fine. But promise me, if there's a way, I want to kill him."

Ryder stares at me long and hard, his deep- set eyes glittering as they narrow. "You understand what you're asking to do? What you want? That's not-"

"I know what it is and I know what it's not and I know it's what I want."

He stares at me long and hard, face a façade of stone but eyes scanning me from head to toe.

"I am choosing who I become," I announce.

He gives a slow nod expression taunt. "Ok then. I'll see what I can do."

I say nothing, holding Ryder steady in my gaze.

"I need you to trust me, poppet."

I still say nothing, forcing myself out of the room and upstairs to find Jax and Rey and convince them of... whatever I need to convince them of at this point. Or convince myself because there are no good choices anymore.

They're both in my bedroom, waiting for me in silence. They've hauled Jax's mattress in from his room, where he now rests on my floor. Rey has thrown himself onto the sofa on the far wall. Even in the darkness, I can see the heavy circles under both their eyes.

"We're going with you?" Rey asks.

I lick my lips. "Yeah," I lie. "We're leaving in the morning. Ryder says get some rest."

The thing is, I'm not leaving in the morning. I'm leaving tonight. If I go to the Risers' compound, it will only delay the inevitable and draw this out longer. I don't know how much more of the anxiety I can take, living each moment in fear, wondering if Elijah hides in the shadows or around the next corner. Never knowing if today will be the day he kills me or kills someone I love. And with that fear, he's getting exactly what he wants, to continue to torture and terrorize me for as long as possible before he puts a bullet through my temple or chops of my head like those mannequins in the forest. I can't live this way but this war will only end with one of us dead, and that won't happen any time soon once I'm back at the Risers' under constant guard like some sort of prisoner. Again. A prisoner again.

When both Jax and Rey have fallen back asleep, their snores deep and steady, I slip from bed, padding across the room in my bare feet to grab my boots and head for the hallway. I wish I could say goodbye, but I have no energy for another argument that will just go around in circles and waste whatever precious time I have left until morning. One last look at them will be all I can have and I'll need them to trust me enough to know I'll come back.

CHAPTER TWENTY-FOUR

As I creep through the house, avoiding creaky floorboards and main halls where I might run into a night guard, my first stop is the kitchen. It's not really functional save a brick, wood burning oven installed on one wall that is now the only useful thing in the space. But it's a central enough location to store our food and supplies in the safehouse. An overgrown garden in the back provides some fresh vegetables and the property has a well to gather water, several buckets of which line the kitchen's quartz counter.

A spare leather backpack rests beside the buckets. I shove two canteens of water inside, followed by a loaf of bread, fresh apples and tomatoes, some candles and flint rocks, a knife and a few other items and food packs I might need. I hope I won't be more than a few days or I'll have starvation to add to my list of problems, but I also can only carry so much and need to leave enough supplies for everyone else in the house.

I still have a handgun Ryder gave to me earlier, but I grab a semi-automatic from the stash in the corner of the room, swinging it onto my shoulder.

"What are you doing?"

My heart leaps into my throat as I spin around to see Rey in the kitchen doorway, the light from my lantern dancing across his face furrowed in confusion.

"Rey, why are you down here?"

"Why are *you* down here. Are you running away? Kelsey,

are you insane?"

"You're following me around? Am I that much of a prisoner here?" I can't conceal the defensive tone in my voice.

"Watchdog, remember? Now, please, *please* tell me you aren't planning to sneak off into the woods somewhere by yourself to hunt down Elijah."

"I don't have a choice Rey."

"Sure you do. Follow Ryder's plan, go back to the Risers' compound tomorrow, let someone else kill Elijah."

"You and I both know that will never work. He's not going to stop threatening or harming the people I care about until he's dead or until I am. I see no point in dragging this out longer."

"He'll kill you, Kels."

"Or I'll kill him. I'm not that same girl you knew in ROC. Both of us have changed Rey, you've said as much yourself. I can do this. I *need* to do this. I can't continue to be a prisoner anymore. I can't live in fear. If those two things are going to remain constant, then I would have been better off in ROC."

He's silent for a long moment, eyes roving over my face. "Then I'm coming with you."

"You can't. I have to be alone or Elijah will never show himself. He's too cautious knowing he's outnumbered. And besides, I need you here to make sure Jax doesn't do something moronic again."

Rey mouth falls open with mock shock. "Moronic? Jax? Never. Though I am honored you think I make intelligent decisions."

"That's not at all what I said, but you can't come with me either way. I'll be careful. I know what I'm doing."

"What are you doing then?"

"Luring him as far away from here as possible and when he attacks, shoot him square in the forehead like Charlie did to Sawyer."

"I don't like this plan."

"I don't either, but we've run out of options. Elijah will follow me to the ends of the Earth. I cannot continue to live like this, wondering who he will hurt next to get to me. Please trust me. I can do this and I'll be careful. And look, I need you and Jax to both be careful too, ok? There's no telling what Elijah is scheming."

Rey castes me one of his goofy smiles, but the cheer is gone from his eyes, replaced by a mixture of deep exhaustion and frightened anxiety. "Careful is my middle name."

"Your middle name is Austin."

"Well, it could be 'careful'. Up here, it's not like anyone but you would know."

Suddenly overcome with emotion, realizing what I'm about to do and this could be the last time I ever see my best friend, I fling my arms around his waist and bury my face in his chest. He returns the hug, kissing the top of my head and then resting his cheek on my hair. He's solid and strong beneath me and for a few wonderful moments, it's as though nothing has ever changed and I can forget the nightmare I am now living.

"Love you, Kels," he says. Not in the romantic way, but in the way that means we are, and always will be, best friends.

"Love you too, Rey "Careful" Zuritsky."

Slipping away, he caresses my cheek with the back of his hand. "Go take care of that red-haired jackass. I'll be here waiting when you get back, and I expect his head on a stick."

I smile. "Maybe I'll even put a bow on it. Like a birthday present."

His face screws up, nose wrinkling. "Come on, now you're just being creepy."

I laugh softly. Readjusting my supply bag and my loaded

gun, I give him the most confident smile my nerves will allow.

"Promise me," he says, "that you'll come back."

I pause for a moment and then with my free hand, I unclasp my mother's necklace, giving it one last longing glance. I extend it to Rey, coiling it into his palm, the silver glittering in the dim candlelight.

"That was my mother's. It was one of the last things she wore and requested my father give it to me when I turned eighteen. It's all I have of her. Keep it safe, because now I have to come back for it."

Rey tightens his grip on the tiny silver pendant. "Ok."

With a final nod, I slip out the side door of the kitchen, scanning the darkness for any sign of guards before darting across the vacant, overgrown front yard and toward the woods, making a point of circling wide through the perimeter just inside the tree line and heading for the macabre display of mannequins Elijah set up, knowing he prowls somewhere nearby.

The dark lantern bangs against my leg, I can't light it until I'm far enough from the safehouse no one will see the flame. The leather bag slaps at my back and the larger gun hangs bulky and awkward around my shoulder. I try to focus on those mundane kinds of things inside of the path on which I'm about to embark. Like when I left ROC, there will be no turning back.

I put on a brave face for Rey's benefit, and to convince him to stay, but the truth is that I'm terrified. I'm terrified to leave the safety of the house, even if Elijah's made it inside, and I'm even more frightened to leave Jax and Rey behind. I don't know what will happen next. I'm not even sure what I want to happen next, but I can't stay at the safehouse and I definitely can't stay at the Risers' compound and put all of those people at risk.

My decision is for the best, I can't argue that. I need my

friends, especially Jax and Rey, to be safe. In a best-case scenario, this will all be over in a few days and things can return to whatever definition of normal we have until we attack ROC. Maybe after all this, everyone will be so grateful we survived the League and Sawyer and Elijah, we'll leave ROC alone.

And then I wish I had never left ROC. Charlie's compound wouldn't be a charred wasteland, Daniel would be alive, Charlie's people wouldn't have been fractured by opposing views over what to do with a Sub, Jax would be... Jax, Rey would be living on his own in the woods and all those people who died in our war with the League; all because of me; would never have been killed. All I've done is brought death and destruction in my wake because I was too childish and immature to overcome grief. I can't continue to allow that to happen.

"I should have just married stupid Wyatt Walker," I grumble to the darkened forest, as I climb over a thick fallen log slippery with early morning dew. Wyatt sucks, but compared to Elijah, he would have been prince charming.

It's too late though. I played a betting game, others have paid the price. I tried to run from the Gamble, but in its own way, it followed right behind. I guess we can't escape the outcome of our choices, no matter how hard we try.

Now I face them head on. It's time to grow up and begin to fix all the problems I've caused. I'll start with Elijah and once that's over, and if I survive, I need to decide between Jax or Rey. I know I said I was waiting until after ROC, but I can't do this to them anymore. It isn't fair. Perhaps I shouldn't be with either until I figure out who I am and what I want and I choose to stop running and hiding from the things I'm too afraid to tackle. Maybe it means I am never with either of them at all. Looking at it now, I guess I was too young to fall in love and take on the responsibilities it requires.

It'll break my heart, and their hearts too, but really, we're already broken anyway. What's another chip at this point?

Both of them are good looking and so full of life and personality, they'll be ok. They'll love again and then all three of us can be friends and someday we'll be thirty years old laughing at all of this.

* * *

As the sun peeks over the horizon and wanders through its daily path, I spend the entire trip in a constant state of unease. Every shadow is Elijah lying in wait. Every rustle in the bushes is his final attack. Every tree branch tugging on my shirt is part of an elaborate trap. Tense and on edge, my gaze whips back and forth through the trees, and dense underbrush lining the almost invisible path. My heart hammers and hands shake and if one more creature startles me, I might throw up and pass out from the fear.

Any confidence I had with this plan is gone within the first hour as I force my feet to continue onward. I am completely alone. If Elijah follows me, this would be the perfect time for him to attack and I remind myself over and over again that I don't think he will. He's going to bid his time. He's going to see where I go and devise a scheme to torture me. He doesn't just want me dead, he wants me begging for it. That can't happen if he fires a bullet through my head in the middle of the woods, there's no enjoyment for him in doing that. Still, I need him to wait long enough until I get to my destination. I need to be in familiar territory if I am to win this battle.

By dusk, fatigued to the point of almost collapsing and my nerves so tattered I've gone numb, I arrive at the mangled gates of Charlie's old compound.

The stone wall still stands with its barbed wire top, mostly untouched by the fire, but as I venture beyond the damaged gates, my heart sinks. Nearly all the buildings have become nothing more than charred, blackened rubble; the long school house Nadia was so happy to go to, the food warehouse, Charlie's little yellow farm house, all gone and replaced by piles of ruins. The weapons' stash had been raided and the metal walls of the building bashed and beaten until they collapsed in on themselves. Even the grassy areas and gardens were trampled and ripped apart, so the once colorful landscape is now a slush pile of mud and rocks and debris.

A place that had stood for over a hundred years, providing shelter and protection to so many people, reduced to almost nothing.

Because of me.

I try to shove aside the guilt, I have no time for it, not while Elijah lays in wait, but it gnaws at me anyway. Charlie's compound is one more reminder of all the destruction I've caused because I wanted to see the sky for one ridiculous second.

At the back corner of the property, some of the wooden cabins still stand, the League probably figured they were already so damaged, what was the point in setting them ablaze? Cabin number thirteen is among those select few that survived.

"And I have come full circle," I mutter staring at the tiny, wooden rectangle with a hole in its roof. The same cabin in which I was held prisoner when I first arrived on the surface, Jax and Daniel my guards. Now, when I need them most, one's dead and the other is miles away. Gazing in dismay at the dilapidated cabin before me, I take note of the rotted and moldy wood panels coated in a layer of dark soot. I would have been perfectly happy never seeing it again.

Easing open the flimsy door, I find the space exactly as I left it with the rickety bed in one corner, a bucket-turned-chamber pot in another and the chair placed beside the door. There's even a pile of torn roof shingles on the floor on the opposite side from my failed escape attempt that seems like a lifetime ago.

Dropping my pack and gun to the floor beside the bed, I

notice brown spots on the wood slats and realize they're droplets of my blood from when Jax cut out the tracker in my arm. Subconsciously, I rub my fingers over the raised scar across my barcode. I can't believe it was only a month ago. So much has changed. I've changed. People have died, Rey has returned from the dead. It seems surreal, like a dream. Or a terrible nightmare. Or both, I guess.

My head spins and I lay on the bed, closing my eyes to clear my mind. I need to be focused and ready. Whatever I'm feeling I need to use it to fuel my hatred of Elijah. He's smart and cunning and far more adept at battle than I'll ever be. I am certain he saw me runaway from the safehouse and has followed. There's no doubt in my mind he was watching, waiting to see what I did next so he can execute his plan.

But I will not let him win. I will not let him take any more lives. I'll avenge all those deaths; Daniel, Ethan, the ROC prisoners murdered before my eyes, even Ashlynn because despite her betrayal, she never deserved what Elijah did to her.

I stare at the weathered rafters of the ceiling. Black soot from the fire has collected in the dust and cobwebs overhead. The smell still hangs in the air even all these weeks later, combined with the scents of damp wood and decaying plants. This place is no longer a sanctuary. It has now become a graveyard of withered wildlife and vacant ruins.

I miss Jax and Rey horribly and feel vulnerable without them here. I know it's for the best and they're safe, but it doesn't change the fact I feel alone, more than I've ever felt. I feel the way I did when I sat in the dark tunnel of ROC, trapped between a past I all but destroyed and a future that very well might destroy me. But I find solace in the fact that one way or the other, in a few days it will be done. One way or another, I won't have to be afraid anymore.

CHAPTER TWENTY-FIVE

For three days I've lived in the compound, jumping at every shift in the tree branches, startling at every tiny noise. I've rationed my food and water, but eventually it will run out. I've slept with the semi-automatic at my side, the handgun under my pillow and a knife in my boots. I've slept in my boots so I can run out of here at a moment's notice.

And still no sign of Elijah. For three entire days.

A part of me wonders if maybe he really didn't follow me. Maybe he's left me to my own devices knowing I'll starve to death on my own or be forced to go crawling back to the safehouse. Maybe that's all part of his plan or none of it and I don't even know what to think anymore because I'm so exhausted, I can't get my head to work right anymore.

Today the world is grey, the sky threatening rain and a drop in temperature causing a dense fog to form. It twists and hovers through the trees, obscuring anything more than a few feet away and giving the woods an eerie, uncomfortable feel. The drab color reminds me of ROC and its monotonous steely grayness, and I find myself breathing heavier, as if those prison walls are closing around me.

I need fresh air so I force myself up from the squeaking bed and step outside. I veer towards the front of the compound, blocking out the damage that pains me to see and heading for the main gates to survey the forest for any sign of that red-haired psychopath.

One of the gates was badly dented by the League when they infiltrated the walls, and now hangs lopsided on its hinges, unable to fully open or close. A vine has woven it's way through the bars, twisting up the metal to reach the sky.

A pile of rocks fallen from the top of the wall rests just outside the broken gate. From the rubble, a sapling has grown, no taller than four feet and boasting only six branches and a scattering of tiny green leaves. I reach through the bars of the gate and run my fingers over a leaf; cool and smooth against my skin.

Allowing my eyes to float over the dark, still woods, I shudder as if I know Elijah watches me; stalking and plotting. I can feel his malicious gaze boring into me, the barrel of his gun leveled with my head, and it's all I can do to not turn and run back to the comfort of my cabin.

But he's not going to shoot me. Not here, like this. That much I know with certainty. He's going to want something much more intricate and painful. Something he can drag out. This is a hunting game for him, and I am the prey.

Suddenly a frustration and rages wells up from inside the anxiety. I shouldn't be here. I shouldn't be afraid of the woods I was once so happy to see and hating the world I was once willing to die to experience. I should be with Jax and Rey and Nadia back at the Risers' compound enjoying everything the surface has to offer and the freedom that comes with it.

"Come out you damn coward!" I scream, my shrill voice surprising even myself. "I know you're there! Come out and let's finish this! I'm right here you disgusting monster!"

The trees remain silent and unmoving, the fog dense and flat. I scan the foliage for any hint of red hair because if I catch even one glimpse, I'll attack him right now. I'll crash through these woods and rip him apart with my bare hands if it means this can end today.

In anger, I pluck a loose rock from the wall and hurl it into the underbrush. Leaves rustle and branches crack as it hops and rolls away from sight, frightening a small squirrel.

"Hey, kid!" someone calls, causing my stomach to hollow out with fear. I flip around, hands balled into fists at my sides, to see Ryder strolling toward me from the direction of the former weapons storehouse. At first I think I am hallucinating, staring at him with my mouth agape and eyes blinking in surprise.

"What are you doing?" he demands.

"Ryder, what… how… what are *you* doing?"

"Making sure you don't end up dead."

I utter confusion, I search around the compound to see if more people appear; Nole or Rey or even Jax.

"It's just me. I followed you when you left the safehouse."

I face Ryder again, a look of incredulity plastered on my face. "You saw me leave?"

"You gave up too easily. That last night when you agreed to go back to the Risers'. I knew you'd be up to somethin' so I packed up a bag of my own and waited in the woods. Sure enough, there you went, crashin' through the forest tryin' to get yourself killed so I followed and hid myself in that wrecked dump over there to keep an eye on you."

Anger swirls inside me and I clench my jaw, teeth barred. "You're the reason my plan hasn't worked."

"Oh yeah? And what exactly was the plan? Stay here till you starve? Or until you're so weak Elijah can take his pick of how to kill you? What were you gonna do here alone?"

"Nothing!" I snap. "It doesn't even matter now because you've ruined it!"

Shoving past him. He grabs my arm, whirling me to face him again.

"I didn't ruin anything," he says, voice low as he leans toward me.

I jerk free of Ryder's grasp and when he reaches for me a second time, I smack his hand away. "Leave me alone!"

"Hey, chill out. What's up with you?"

Fisting my hands into my hair, I emit a growl of rage. "I hate him! I hate Elijah and none of this is fair! I didn't do anything to him. He kidnapped me. He killed people. He started this war and now I'm supposed to spend every moment in fear and sit around waiting for him to finish it? Well, then come finish it!" I scream into the woods again, my voice straining and cords of veins popping in my neck. My breath comes ragged and heavy and I realize I'm trembling all over with fury.

Ryder, arms crossed, watches me rant and rave and stomp my feet, a look of boredom across his features. "You done?"

"No!" I bark marching back and forth, boots pounding the earth. "It's not fair!"

"Fair? Did someone tell you life was fair? Cause, I'm gonna tell you right now, you were lied to."

I stop and glare. "And that's supposed to help me right now?"

His eyes widen and he feints concern. "You wanted help? Coulda fooled me since you ran off all by yourself into the woods with some sort of death wish."

I groan in frustration and grip my hair again as if I'm going to rip it out at the root. "No. I want... my life to be normal."

"Define normal."

Dropping my arms to my sides, I gaze around, taking in the fog and the trees and the grey sky overhead, the crumpling wall and the decimated compound. It's begun to drizzle and I didn't even notice, tiny drops striking my face like little pin pricks.

"I want to be safe. I want to be with my friends. I want-"

"You want to be back in ROC?"

"No! No. Not that." I sigh. "I wasn't really safe there either, not with the Gamble and the rations and everything else. I guess my life has never been normal."

"Nor has anyone else's. Normal doesn't exist. Normal is some random, elusive adjective we use to define our opinions and ideals. In the old world, I've heard it was used to sell people crap they didn't need so someone else could bathe in gobs of money. I dunno, but stop expectin' normal, it's an illusion that will disappoint you every time."

"Then what am I supposed to expect?"

"Nothin'. You'll rarely get it anyway. Just press forward with the path you have and eventually you'll get where you're goin'. Now, are you finished actin' the fool?"

With embarrassment, I jam my hands into my back pockets and kick at the dust on the ground.

Ryder grips my shoulder in one thick hand. "Come on. Now you know I'm here I don't need to hide anymore. I might as well go back to the cabin with you and keep each other company. We can figure out the next course of action in the mornin'."

* * *

The following morning, I rise with the sun, its brightness cheery and energizing after a day of gloomy skies and chilly rain. The change in weather, and after releasing some of my anger and stress in the outburst yesterday, my mood has tempered.

Ryder snores on the floor in the corner, one hand on the barrel of his own gun. After my initial fury, I found myself grateful he's here. Last night I actually got some real sleep and feel energized, even though I know once he awakes, he's going to demand I go back to the Risers' with him. Maybe I should. This entire runaway and face off with Elijah alone was dumb. It didn't even work.

Intending to take one last look at the forest, I quietly exit the cabin, leaving my weapons because I'll only be a minute.

Making my way to the gates, I let my eyes flicker over the forest, the trees still damp from last night's rain, droplets shimmering on their leaves like diamonds. Everything smells crisp and fresh. Even the sky seems like a brighter shade of blue, as if the world has been repainted and touched-up and restored to its former glory.

All remains quiet and normal. For all we know, Elijah was never here at all. He could be back at the safehouse still terrorizing my friends and the idea forms a lump in my throat. It's time to wake Ryder and go back, figure out what to do from here.

I scan the quiet forest again before turning on my heels.

And there it is, dangling on the little sapling just outside the gates to my right shoulder, the silver glittering in the early morning sunlight. At first my brain doesn't register and I shift closer to inspect thinking it must be trash swept up in the branches from last night's storm. However, once recognition dawns, my insides drop out and my knees turning to jelly. I have to hang onto the gate to stop myself from toppling over, the rust scratching against my palm. The world around me fades, the silver piece of jewelry all I can see.

My mother's necklace, the simple little heart that has survived so much and made it so far. The necklace I gave Rey before I left, knowing he would never let it out of his possession until I returned. Now it swings on the sapling, as if placed there only a few minutes ago.

Hair rises on the back of my neck. Trembling, I slide

around the gate and tip-toe outside the compound, examining the area for any sign of Elijah, but knowing wherever he lurks, I'll never see him.

With pale, hesitant fingers, I lift the chain of the necklace, unwinding it from the tree. The metal is still warm to the touch and I shudder because it wasn't Rey who held it last.

Attached to the necklace, wound into its chain, is a slip of paper, another of Elijah's notes. My stomach lurches as I disentangle and unroll it.

You want this over? So do I. If you want to see either of them again, you have till noon to come unarmed to where this all started. If you're late, one dies. If you attempt to bring anyone with you, I kill them both.

There are three ways today will end. One; I don't go and he kills one of them and I die because I can't live without both of them. Two; I tell Ryder and we go together and Elijah finds out and kills both of them and I die because I can't live without both of them. Three; I follow Elijah's orders and go alone and he kills me and ends this all. Any which way I play Elijah's twisted game, today my luck runs out.

The note tumbles from my fingers, floating to the dirt where it rests on the stone wreckage piled there.

I have to go though. Alone. I have no choice. And I have to hurry because according to the sun, it's almost noon. Casting a pitiful look at the burned compound and poor little cabins making a final stand in the ashes, I see Ryder stalking toward me from the cabins.

"Poppet, don't!"

He knows.

I can't let him follow me, I can't let him know where I'm going because I can't put Jax and Rey at risk.

Slamming my shoulder against the broken gate, I force it towards its mate, shoving the two as close together as their warped frames will allow. Ryder's feet pound on the damp earth, drawing him closer and closer and I'm almost out of time. Yanking a large limb from the ground, I jam it through the handles of the gates, locking them in place.

Then I turn and bolt into the tree line. The branch won't stop Ryder, but it will buy me a few minutes. If I move quickly enough, I can disappear into the woods before he makes it out of the compound. I only need to be a few minutes ahead of him to save the boys I love. Once I'm there, Elijah won't draw this out any further. A few minutes head start is all I need. Ryder will be pissed at me, but I'll be dead so it won't really matter.

Charging through the underbrush, ducking low branches, leaping over logs and dodging thorns and rocks, I run and run, zig-zagging through the woods, until my lungs burn and legs tingle with sharp aches and cramps. Leaning against a tree I pant and gasp as sweat beads down my skin, the rising humidity of the late-spring morning making it hard to breathe.

My ears prick for any sound of boots or motion along the thick shrubbery. Confirming Ryder isn't following, or at least not in the correct direction, I check my bearings. I'm pretty sure I'm headed the right way, but I've only gone through here once before and that was at night and I wasn't really paying attention because I had a gun at my back. I can't be wrong though. I have no time for screw ups. Then I second guess my destination anyway since the note wasn't specific. I'm only guessing at the location Elijah has given.

No choice. I have no choice.

I need to act now and pray I'm not wrong. Shoving off the tree, I take off again, winding along the overgrown, nearly invisible pathway. It's useless to look for clues or signs of someone coming through here before me. Elijah's grown up in this type of environment, he knows how to move through the forest without leaving a trail. He won't make this easy for me.

I run my fingers over the chain of my mother's necklace still wrapped around my hand, tangled into my fingers. Stopping once more, my heart pounding from both fear and exertion, I link the chain around my neck, fingering the delicate charm. Somehow, it gives me strength. My mother wore it until her final minutes. I will too. Maybe, if I still have a teensy bit of luck left, I can have Rey or Jax pass it on to Nadia when I'm gone. It will be the only thing I leave behind in this world.

And fading memories of course, but eventually those will be gone too, no further remains of my mark on this world, the fact I was here and I tried my damnedest to live. I will be like the towering buildings that once littered the surface, tall and strong and invincible. So many of those are gone now, not so much as the hint of their foundations remaining, as if they never existed at all.

The idea of my imminent death strikes me, punching me in the gut and causing me to double over. A strangled sob escapes my throat and I fall to my knees on the damp earth.

I die today. Today. No more sunrises and no more sunsets. No more hopes or dreams or plans of a future where I could be happy someday. This is it, my final hour, leaving behind so many things undone.

It's not like I've never considered my death before. Living in ROC, reminders of death are everywhere, especially on Gamble days. And there was my failed suicide attempt after Rey's number was chosen, but even that didn't seem real at the time, I was so consumed by grief.

"All I ever wanted was to see the sky," I whisper to myself. Tears obscure my vision, but I wipe them away to gaze up at the sky; blue and brilliant and vast. Was it worth it? Was the sky worth dying over?

Yes. I had wanted it to be the last thing I saw and, after all of this, it still will be. Drawing in deep breaths and shoving to my feet. It can't be much farther now.

CHAPTER TWENTY- SIX

In the last few yards, I know I picked the correct location because I see three sets of footprints in the soft, damp earth, one marching confident and unwavering, two stumbling behind, the toes of the boots sliding against the mud. I hope they're ok, Jax and Rey, I can't bear to face my last minutes of life if I find them hurt.

Calming my pace, I close my eyes, willing the shaking in my limbs to subside before I walk into Elijah's trap. I have no idea what I will find, I have no weapon, I have nothing but myself. But that's what Elijah wants. Just me.

Notching my chin higher and steeling my gaze, I march the last several feet, brush aside a leafy branch, skirt a prickly bush and step into the small clearing surrounding the external, metal door to ROC. Where I once emerged from. Where this all began the moment I set foot on the surface.

I haven't seen the door in weeks. The rusted metal barrier and faded "Danger" sign seem insignificant and harmless set into a hillside of grass and moss and wildflowers. If I didn't know any better, I'd assume it once belonged to a long-abandoned government building filled now with nothing but dust and dirt and stale air. Maybe a few dead rodents. My father's gun rests somewhere around here, but I'll never find it, if it will even work after a month of exposure to the elements. Like me, the gun will never leave this place.

However, it's not the door or the thought of the gun that

holds my attention. In front of the solitary, impenetrable entrance to ROC, Jax and Rey kneel, wrists bound behind their backs and mouths gagged.

Rey looks okay, healthy and strong, just like I left him, only a few fresh marks and bruises that had to be Elijah's doing. Jax on the other hand, appears weak and sickly, his pale skin dotted with perspiration. A circle of blood seeps into his T-shirt where his cauterized wound has begun to weep and drain from too much physical exertion.

But they are both alive and I exhale a deep breath of relief. With Elijah, I'm never sure what I will find.

As I step into the clearing, both of them look up, eyes widening as they strain against their bindings, screams muffled. Jax jerks his head no, face imploring me to run.

I hold up my empty hands. "It's ok. I know what I'm doing here. I haven't been tricked or walked into a trap. I know how this ends."

Behind them stands Elijah, red hair shining in the midday sun. In his hand glints the metal of a handgun, which he alternates between the back of Jax and Rey's heads. I swallow the lump in my throat, raising my own hands higher.

"Elijah, I came alone, just like you asked."

"Good," he sneers. "I was convinced you were going to do something stupid."

I take a couple steps forward until I stand less than six feet from Jax and Rey. I can almost touch them. "I followed your instructions. I'm here alone and unarmed. No one else is coming. You can let them go now. I'm the one you want."

"Stop," he orders, aiming the gun at me and I freeze in my tracks. Then he smiles, teeth glittering like fangs, hair wild about his head, skin smudged and smeared with dirt from his brief time living in the woods. He doesn't even look human anymore. "I'm not letting them go just yet."

I grit my teeth, anger flashing across my face. "What do you want from me then? To go with you somewhere? To kill myself? Whatever it is, I'll do it. You don't need to use Jax or Rey anymore."

Elijah chuckles, sinister and bone-chilling. "Actually, I do need them. I'm going to make a very generous deal with you. In fact, it will be the same deal my grandfather gave to Charlie."

"You mean your mother," I say.

His features contort and darken. "She is *not* my mother. She abandoned me because she was too afraid to do what needed to be done. She turned her back on her family because she couldn't make the hard choices in life. But let's see if you can. Can you make hard choices, Kelsey?"

"I'm here aren't I? Despite knowing you're going to kill me."

"Oh, I'm not going to kill you. I mean, I wanted to. A part of me still does, but I won't. That would be too simple, too easy for you. You don't deserve easy, not after all the trouble you've caused."

A fresh wave of dread washes over me. "You said, in your note, if I came alone and unarmed you wouldn't hurt them."

Now his chuckles turn to laughter, a cold, empty sound erupting from deep in his chest. "All this time and you still don't know what to look for in the things I don't say. Read between the lines, Kelsey! Reading comprehension is your friend. I said I wouldn't hurt *one* of them. Doesn't mean I won't hurt the other, and you're going to help. Today, you are going to walk out of here alive because you are going to make a choice. One that will mean I never bother you again, but one that will haunt you for the rest of your pathetic, dismal life. You are going to choose whether dear Jax here dies, or whether Rey does."

If words held actual, physical force, I'd be dead right now. Instead, my arms fall to my sides as my mouth drops open, all energy and confidence draining from my body.

"What?" I choke.

"It's simple, really. You're going to choose between Jax or Rey. I mean, isn't that what you've been trying to do for weeks now? One of them dies, one of them lives. Which one will it be?"

I can't breathe. I can't think. I can't even stand up anymore as the world spins and tumbles, tossing me to the ground on all fours. I curl the grass between my fingers, gagging and wrenching. My hair cascades around my face as I rock on my hands and knees, unable to grasp what Elijah has said.

"No. No. I will never choose that," I whisper.

"That isn't one of the options I've given you. It's either Jax, or it's Rey."

"No!"

"Then I kill both of them!"

"NO!" I scream, finding the strength to haul myself back to my feet, swaying and dizzy as desperate panic sets in. I look to Jax and then to Rey, both hopeless and helpless between Elijah and me. Their looks of despair weight on me, heavy and constricting.

"Kill me!" I cry, my voice shrill and desperate as I beat my chest. "Kill me instead!"

It's what I was prepared for. It's why I came here. To die, not to... not for this.

Around his gag, Jax screams in protest, struggling against the ropes that bind his arms. Rey, clear blue eyes wide, shakes his head so violently that his neck may snap. But I don't care about their objections. I'd rather Elijah kill me because if he takes one of them, I'll only die anyway.

"No," Elijah replies, his voice hissed and snarling, more like a feral animal than a man. "Like I said, killing you would make this too easy. I want you to suffer instead. I want you to PAY for what your father and your people did to mine! To everyone on the surface! I want you to pay for what you did to my grandfather and to my home. I want you to pay for all of it."

"I didn't kill Sawyer, and I didn't have anything to do with what's happened on the surface."

His eyes glitter like a demonic beast. "This is your punishment, Sub, so which one is it going to be?"

The gun passes back and forth between Jax and Rey as Elijah trains it on each of them in turn, his wicked stare never leaving my face. My heart rages so bad inside my chest, it might burst through my ribcage. I hear its pounding in my ears, drowning out everything except Elijah's orders.

"Choose!" he screams, features contorting with psychotic rage as he thrusts the gun at Rey.

I shut my eyes. I can't risk looking at one too long and making Elijah think I've made my choice. I can't see their eyes boring into my skull like a bullet of its own as I am forced to decide their fates. One lives, one dies. Either way, one never walks out of this. Either way, I loose. Jax or Rey.

"No!" I sob, unable to draw a full breath as my chest squeezes painfully, crushing my lungs. Opening my eyes again I find Elijah's twisted face, his rage burning through as I plead. "Please, Elijah. Please, don't do this."

My insides rip apart as I stare helplessly at Jax and Rey, both fighting against their restraints with looks of solid determination. Despite everything I've done, the situation they are now in, they both still want to save me. I can't fathom why. I don't deserve them and I definitely don't deserve to be saved.

"Do it," Elijah spits, "or I swear I'll shoot them both."

Tears pour down my cheeks, pooling along my chin before escaping to the ground. I look and the two boys I love, the two who mean more to me in this world than my own life.

Someone will die, that's the only way this will end, with their death and not my own. But I can't choose. I never could. Not over who I love more and certainly not over who should live and who should die. I love them both, I want them both here. Neither deserves this, deserves anything I have done to them. If one dies, a part of me will die too and all I wish is that Elijah would turn that gun on me so this can be over.

"Elijah, I can't. Please don't make me choose."

"Fine. I'll make this easier for you. Let's play a little game." Jamming the gun in the back of Jax's head, Elijah smiles again and it occurs to me he enjoys this. My misery is fun for him and this is nothing more than sadistic entertainment. The thought churns my stomach; that someone can be so rotten and deranged to their very core that they find joy in another's unbearable agony.

Charlie blames herself for what he has become, but this kind of insatiable savagery isn't created, it is born. Somehow, in whatever way our consciousness is constructed, Elijah's didn't mold together properly. He is a demon that should have never been allowed to walk the Earth.

I have no weapon, if I try to overcome Elijah he'll shoot one of them. Ryder... he's my only hope but I have no idea where he is, if he will even arrive on time. If I can just stall Elijah a little longer, if I can just give Ryder a few more minutes, maybe we can still win this. Jax and Rey can live.

"Elijah," I whisper, my tone pleading. "Please. Please don't do this."

Jax doesn't flinch as Elijah's thumb pulls back the hammer, the soft click echoing in the trees as the gun cocks. I feel every muscle in my body contract in fear.

"Einy," Elijah says with a sneer. "Meeny. Miney. Mo." The gun transfers back and forth, back and forth, jabbing into their heads every time. And each time he does, I feel another part of me rupture deep in my soul, as if I am coming undone from the inside out, crumpling and splintering.

"Elijah, stop! Choose me instead. Please choose me!"

His eyes burn into mine, as he continues. "Catch. A tiger. By. His toe."

"Stop!" I scream, voice wavering, cheeks wet with tears as my entire body convulses, nerves unraveling.

"I'll stop when you choose!" He screams. The gun still alternates between them, hovering behind their heads as if it has a mind of its own and can't wait to destroy everything in my world.

"I can't!" I cry.

"Einy. Meeny. Miney."

The gun fires, freezing me, a new scream trapped in my throat as the cracking sound of the shot bounces through the forest, echoing in my ears until I can hear nothing else. I feel it against my bones, rattling my insides and making the blood ice over in my veins. A single noise that has now changed the entire course of my existence in this world.

Suddenly, in the small window of opportunity I'm given, and a large bit of utter insanity because it is all I have left, I'm lunging at Elijah. I hurl myself into his chest, wrapping an arm around his neck and together we tumble to the hard ground. Two more gunshots whip past my head, one taking a chunk of my left earlobe, but in my crimson-tinged wrath, I barely register the fiery pain.

I straddle him, slamming a forearm across his throat. Our noses nearly touch as he looks up at me from the ground. His eyes are devoid of emotion and filled with pure evil, the kind that wants nothing more than to watch the whole world crumble and decay until it is as cold and dead as the evil itself. And even then, he'll never be happy, it will never be enough to feed his heartless madness.

But I am no longer scared. I am... I am... I'm something else entirely; something that I'd never even known slithered inside me, but now it unfurls in the shadows of my mind, a beast awoken from a deep slumber, charging forward to be free.

Twisting his arm, he moves to aim the gun at my temple. I'm not sure I even care anymore, if I even want to continue to live, but I will not die before I kill Elijah. We will go out of this life together. The fear of death that once confined me is gone, giving me the freedom do to what must be done.

A large rock sits beside us, I curl my fingers around it, heavy and solid in my hand. Without so much as a moment of hesitation, I slam it down onto his face. Bone crushes and blood spurts, splattering hot and thick across my skin. He shrieks and tries to recoil in agony, swatting at me and struggling to move away. But I've trapped him between my knees, pinning him to the ground with a strength that doesn't feel human.

I hit him again. And then again. And then again and again and again, screaming in fury as I do so, until the rock is so soaked and saturated with fresh, wet blood, it slips from my grasp and rolls away.

Blood drips from my hands and the sliminess of it coats my face. I taste it on my tongue; salty and metallic. My breath heaves, heart thundering as I look down at what I've done. Elijah is unrecognizable. His features have become nothing more than a bloody, pulpy mess of tattered flesh, mutilated muscle and broken skull. One eye protrudes from its socket and nearly all his teeth are gone. The right side of his face is crushed in like a deflated ball, his nose torn away and one ear connected only by grisly strands of cartilage.

I know he's dead, and now I have become a monster because killing Elijah was easy. I am happy he is dead. I feel no remorse or guilt or anything other than a surge of satisfaction that I've taken him out of this world. I woke the caged beast dozing in the pits of my soul, and now it is a part of me.

Turning back to Jax and Rey, I see only one still kneeling, twisting to stare, eyes horrified above the gag in his mouth. Beside him, the other boy lies supine on the forest floor, a clean bullet hole through the back of his head, blood spilling into the earth. My heart twists and struggles before bursting apart as though it has been squeezed in a vise.

I don't know why, but all I can picture is my crystal water glass smashing on the floor the night I argued with my father about marrying Wyatt. Like the glass, whatever walls I had once placed in my mind to protect myself, now come tumbling down, shattering into millions of fragments never to be whole again. I can almost hear them splintering, a tinkling of glass with a cascade of glittering shards.

I feel my soul flee, no longer able to deal with the anguish slicing though my body like razors. The grief; the mist of a demon; swirls and grows until it fills my veins. Monsters and demons, it is all I have become.

The darkness swarms inside me, devouring every inch of my being, consuming me and changing me and dragging me into its black abyss.

And I welcome it. I loved him and now he is dead. I want to be dead too.

ACKNOWLEDGEMENT

Ok, two-thirds of the way done this thing and so far people are still reading! Now the pressure is on to make the third book amazing, especially after I've left everyone hanging at the end of this one. Sorry, not sorry. Now, who is Team Jax and who is Team Rey?

I again need to thank my cover artist, Katie Rasinski at KT Razz Designs for making the book look stunning. No one would buy it if it weren't for the awesome cover.

Of course, thank you to my family for being my biggest supporters and being the first ones to buy each book, even though some of you have already read it four times and seen at least three different endings.

I also need to thank a few friends; the TL/DR FB group chat (or whatever the chat name has changed to by this point) for all of your enouragement, insipiration or general celebratory emojies. Also, as promised, thank you Mac Casey for your expertise and helping to prove me right. I also want to thank everyone who has shared the book, word of mouth is the best marketing and means the world to me!

Thank you to my five Gamble ambassadors for putting word out there about the series, I hope you enjoy this second one.

Lastly, thank you to all my readers and fans. I promise not to make you wait too long for the ending of this trilogy.

Now, I beg; please consider leaving me a review on Amazon, Goodreads, Facebook or anywhere else. It costs you nothing but a minute or two of your time and becomes invalueable to me. As an independent author, I don't have the luxury of a fancy publishing house with a large marketing budget and experienced staff to make my book a hit. I rely on you, my readers and fans, for every review, share, social media shoutout or whatever other support you can give!

ABOUT THE AUTHOR

Kathryn Jacques

Raised in Baltimore, Maryland, Kathryn Jacques graduated with a BFA in Dance Performance from Towson University. She performed professionally as both a classical and contemporary dancer for several years.

Upon retiring from the stage, Kathryn transitioned into TV and film acting where she appeared in numerous TV shows, commercials and independent films. She starred in the 2016 feature film Soul Fray, which premiered at the Cannes Film Festival. It was during her down time on sets when she returned to her childhood love of writing, and eventually The Gamble series was born.

Kathryn still lives in Maryland with her husband and their two daughters.

BOOKS BY THIS AUTHOR

The Gamble

Book 1
Now available

Redemption

Book 3
Coming Summer 2021